THE FALLEN TREES ARE ALSO THE FOREST

ALEJANDRA KAMIYA is a Japanese-Argentine writer. Born in Buenos Aires, she has published three collections of short stories and won numerous awards for her writing, including the Horacio Quiroga Award and the Konex Award. *The Fallen Trees Are Also the Forest* is her first book to be translated into English.

DANIEL HAHN is a writer, editor, and translator with around a hundred books to his name. Recent books include *If This Be Magic: the unlikely art of Shakespeare in translation*, and translations of novels from Guatemala, Brazil, Mexico and Angola.

THE FALLEN TREES ARE ALSO THE FOREST

ALEJANDRA KAMIYA

TRANSLATED FROM THE SPANISH
BY DANIEL HAHN

PUSHKIN PRESS

Pushkin Press
Somerset House, Strand
London WC2R 1LA

The Fallen Trees Are Also the Forest was first published as *Los árboles caídos también son el bosque* by Bajo La Luna in Buenos Aires, 2015

First published by Pushkin Press in 2026

ISBN 13: 978-1-80533-491-0

A CIP catalogue record for this title is available from the British Library

The authorised representative in the EEA is eucomply OÜ, Pärnu mnt. 139b-14, 11317, Tallinn, Estonia, hello@eucompliancepartner.com, +33757690241

Designed and typeset by Tetragon, London
Printed and bound in the United Kingdom by Clays Ltd, Elcograf S.p.A.

Pushkin Press is committed to a sustainable future for our business, our readers and our planet. This book is made from paper from forests that support responsible forestry.

www.pushkinpress.com

1 3 5 7 9 8 6 4 2

For Kenta

CONTENTS

PERFECT
BREAKFAST

You won't wait for the light to slip through the window. You will look at Takashi sleeping beside you. It's good he's resting, you'll think, because he has a long day of work ahead. You'll get up from the futon without a sound, and walk light-footed across the tatami to the kitchen, and you'll dress there so as not to tear Hiro and Takashi's paper sleep.

A perfect breakfast calls for fresh fish and the freshest of all is around the Tsukiji market. It's mackerel season.

You'll take the train to Tsukiji for a perfect mackerel.

There, every single one will look lovely to you. That blue shimmer, the tiger stripes on black that is wet, always wet, like a recollection that never dries, a memory of the sea.

You will shut your eyes, and choose. You won't allow yourself to be carried away by what you see alone.

You'll travel back home with the perfect mackerel in a bag, hoping for no delays. That would be a loss of freshness. A crack in the smoothness of your plans.

Back home, you will slice the mackerel in half and salt it, so it retains the spirit of the sea. You'll leave the rice to soak, having washed your hands with that coconut soap Mariko gave you. How lucky you are. How many Japanese women wash their face and hands in the morning with coconut soap?

You will imagine a beach like the ones in travel-agent advertisements and focus your imagination up at the tips of the palm trees: you'll see the coconuts, the ones they used for making the soap so that your hands could be soft this morning. You will wish that something of this beach and this coconut whiteness might pass into the rice through your hands as you wash it and leave it to rest.

The resting is important. In all things.

To make the miso shiru, you will scent the water with small, dried anchovies. You will imagine the dance of the coconut's sweetness with the anchovies' salty taste. As if that same sea that caresses the feet of the palms were doing it now in Tokyo, in your house.

You won't put many anchovies in the water because otherwise that dance of flavors will turn into a battle.

Next you go to open the natto, and the packet of nori, the one you saved up to buy. Nori of a perfect blackness, death-like, without the green glints of more common seaweed.

There's something arrogant in that gesture and you will be embarrassed, but the idea of a perfect breakfast will once again convince you that you did the right thing, that just a single component of a different quality would mean the work on all the others was wasted.

Which is also why you will use the tea from the first flush, that tea from the south of Japan. You'll take the water off the stove before it boils, you'll just moisten the leaves, and after pouring on the water you will let them rest. They'll stretch and their flavor will be allowed to emerge, their scent, their green essence in your gray kitchen. You will go to your son's room. You'll stay there a little while, kneeling beside the futon watching his breaths. Truly you could spend all the time in the world here, let the breakfast rot in the kitchen and the rest of the meaningless world fall apart out there and you'd just keep on kneeling beside Hiro's futon. As if he belonged to you and not to the waiting world, of which he is just one more cog.

You'll put a hand on his skinny little shoulder. The boy will say: "Hey," and you'll answer in a voice neither loud nor quiet that it's time to get up.

He will rub his eyes and say: "OK, mamá," and then he'll pull the covers back up, to laze about for just one more minute. Then you will come back to the kitchen and listen as Hiro and your husband ready themselves for their days that are filled with obligations, the way trees are filled with fruit or flowers.

You will mix the mustard into the natto: a sword dance. A sharp tinkling in your nose.

You will place everything on the table with the same care as every other morning, only now seeking something different.

Not one angle must be out of tune, not one color must clash or be erased, they should flow toward Hiro and his papá.

The scents should seduce like something hidden. The ordering should be pleasant like the voices of the elevator girls in department stores.

You will place a small flower down beside the natto dish. Almost an act of vanity that you will be unable to avoid. A sign, perhaps.

Your husband and Hiro will kneel beside the breakfast. You will enjoy watching them eat. Hiro, a little ungainly as if still nestled in sleep, will rub his face with the back of the hand in which he's holding the ohashi.

You will crack an egg into his bowl. A whole sun will spread across a small rice world.

You will see Hiro finish waking up as he chews, and you'll see him realize that this is a perfect breakfast. Your husband will eat everything down to the last grain of rice, every last bit of the natto, every last fiber of the mackerel and he will nod while he does it.

"Oishi," Hiro will say, and you'll be content and you will thank him, just tipping your head and smiling more with your eyes than with your lips that do not part. "Oishi," the boy will say again, and you'll feel a puffer fish in your chest. Your husband will nod again.

The table will be left empty. Only the bowls, cups, small dishes, all empty as skeletons. And the flower, open like a yelling mouth. Mute of meaning in its beauty.

Hiro will say he's got English class and he'll race from the table.

Your husband will wait a little, as if he were resting, like the rice, like the tea. You will rinse your hands to say good-bye to them. You will use your coconut soap one more time.

Hiro will have his backpack and his baseball cap.

You'll tell him to take it off before going into school.

He'll nod and tell you his friend's waiting for him on the next block.

You'll say not to make him wait.

Your husband, already at the door, will tell you before putting on his shoes that it was a perfect breakfast. You'll thank him for that.

Alone in the house, you will clean with great care, as always, only differently. Things can always be better. What a lack of humility it would be not to try.

When you have finished, you go sit beside the oven and open the door, which comes down like a drawbridge.

You'll turn the knob and rest your head on the door as if it were a pillow on which you were going to nap.

The note of apology will have been written already and you'll have left it on the table.

You will think about sun-filled beaches and very tall palm trees. At their tips you will see coconuts and you'll guess at their white insides and their scent.

You'll look at the sea, and feel that strange smell as it comes and goes.

THE REMAINS OF
THE SECRET

Her nakedness does not display parts, those parts that are normally covered. Guillermina's nakedness is like the nakedness of trees in autumn: what it reveals is a lack. With bones standing out, their points protruding here and there, Guillermina has something of the batwing about her, something of the half-opened umbrella.

Belinda, meanwhile, is like a large white loaf of home-made bread.

They dress up.

The prairie land is flat like a sheet, and that is where they go, to write stories onto it.

Belinda shakes her head so that a straight black lock falls over one eye. She is carrying a broken tray on which they have placed empty packs of Jockey Clubs and Parliaments, and two complete cigarettes that Guille lifted from her grandfather that afternoon.

The hoops of Belinda's earrings brush over her rounded shoulders as she looks at herself in the mirror that's tied with wire to the metal plates of the shed. She paints her lips and her mouth is transformed: everything she says with this new red mouth will be important.

Enter the toreador: Guillermina with a black hat, tights, and a violet sash. She has the piece of cloth covering one shoulder. It's the curtain from the kitchen from before. Guille walks as if on a tightrope, one foot lined up with the other. Her lips are slightly tense, as if seeking to hold up the mustache that has been drawn on with a burnt cork. One hand on her waist. She uses the other to doff her hat and she waves a greeting, gazing out into the distance. Just watching how she walks is enough for Belinda to hear the cheering crowds.

"Carmen," says Guille, standing tall. "Come with me up into the mountains. I have a gang. We steal everything. I will give you a life, Carmen." "Ay, torero, but I have a life already," says Belinda, eyes down. "I can give you another," Guillermina insists. "But torero, each person has only one life," says Belinda, rearranging the cigarette packets. "No, Carmen," says Guillermina, spinning her piece of cloth. "We have many of them, like paths. If we do not walk down them, weeds grow and cover them over. Take heart, Carmen, let us go." "Very well, torero," says Belinda, flicking her hair to one side. They look ahead and walk with chins raised. When they play they always have their chins raised. The rest of the time, however, they are lowered and it is their eyes that stand out. Especially Guillermina's, so hungry and so big.

They had read the story of Carmen on the sleeve of a record. Somebody over in the town had thrown away a few of them in shellac and in vinyl and Guille and Belinda had kept them.

They always keep things and with them construct other things. In this world, objects are unconfined and they are transformed. Today's toreador cape was the tablecloth for an Egyptian banquet yesterday, and before that a little baby's blanket from some kind of Greek tragedy. The baby had died and Guille and Belinda created a funeral cortege. At first it looked as though nothing was happening to Guille. She walked silently beside Belinda, who wept and wailed and beat her breast, crushing flowers and tearing at her clothes. Guille, who was the father, walked in silence without moving his arms, until he suddenly dropped straight down onto the ground and Belinda thought he was dead. Belinda did the sign of the cross so quickly they looked like figure eights, one after another, ending with a vigorous kiss on her fingertips, and then another cross, another crooked eight over her forehead, shoulders, and chest.

Then they wondered whether or not it's possible to die of sadness.

"You *can* die of sadness," they said, "and also of love. So really," they said, "you've got to be careful." They thought about señorita Ana. Guille and Belinda were afraid she might die. Even the sums she wrote on the blackboard were saddening. "The bad thing about boyfriends," they had concluded, "is that they leave you."

Guille and Belinda sit together, and together they go and come from the ranch school to the place where Belinda lives. Guillermina's home is closer to the big house and to the sunflowers.

One evening, as it's getting late, Belinda's father comes over to the sink where she's washing the dishes and says:

"You're not to walk back from school with the Cáceres girl anymore." "Why?" asks Belinda, her eyes wide.

Juan Arancibia moves the toothpick around in his mouth and says: "Because you're not to walk back from school with the Cáceres girl anymore."

That night Belinda doesn't think about what she's going to be when she grows up. Belinda is asking herself questions and because she does not answer herself, she doesn't sleep.

When she tells Guillermina about it, her friend says to ignore him, that they'll walk back over the hill, that way nobody will see them and go telling tales to her father.

And finally everything works out for the best, because there on the hill they are building a house.

Each day they add a part and the house grows and it is there to receive them every afternoon.

It is a slow magic, the sort of magic that means when they imagine a wall and say: "From here to here," some real thing does gradually take shape.

When Belinda's mother cooks she always says she does it slowly "so that it doesn't get out of hand." That's what Belinda thinks of as she places branch upon branch.

She likes to do things slowly. She chooses her sticks from the ones Guillermina gathers and fits them together to keep out as much as possible of the light, the rain, the cold. They could fill those holes with mud, make a kind of adobe. Or real adobe, thinks Belinda. She could tell her father, but then he would ask why she wants to know and he'd say something about Cáceres and everything would be ruined.

The house, thinks Belinda, is called The Secret. Secrets are things that keep people inside of them, protecting them or holding them prisoner. Every house could be called that. We move from our parents' secret to establish our own secret with the person we choose.

Belinda chooses Guillermina and together they build a house of windowless walls. When you are old, thinks Belinda, sometimes you find yourself unable to share your secret with anybody, or worse, like Guillermina's grandfather, having to share it with a whole load of people you haven't chosen. Or maybe Guille's grandfather no longer has a secret at all.

Before leaving, they go into the house. The sun is setting and inside there's no light. "I'd like to live here forever," says Guille, with a sigh.

There is a sound of birds.

No, it's one bird. Just one.

It starts to turn cold, as if the cold were falling slowly from the sky over every single thing, and embracing each one before entering and changing it.

"Let's be ghosts, then," says Belinda, because Guille has said she would like to stay forever.

Guille smiles and puts her hands in her lap. She looks at the light that is just barely coming in through the hole that is the house's door.

The song from the sole bird is gradually going out.

There's something of a goodbye in that time of the afternoon.

They know they need to go back, so they get to their feet, pick up their exercise books and pencils.

"Women love their homes," says Belinda as they walk over the hill. "Not my mom," says Guille, dragging a stick. "Other women love other things," says Belinda now. "Not my mom," says Guillermina, striking the path with the stick. "Some women don't love anything," says Belinda, trying to sound convincing. She looks at her friend, who tosses the stick away. As far away as she can.

The next day they learn that María Antonia has had her baby. While the blackboard fills up with letters, Guillermina remembers María Antonia's belly. Several times they had put a doll under their clothing to play at carrying a baby in their bellies. But when Guille saw María Antonia she thought they'd made a big mistake doing it like that, it had been like trying to represent an egg by drawing the outline of a baby chick. Guille remembers it being more like a melon, a ball, a moon, an egg, a fruit, cupped hands. To take away its roundness is to take away the whole thing.

"What are you thinking about, Guillermina?" asks señorita Ana. "Nothing," Guille says, and she starts copying the letters into her exercise book. What's round is complete, that is what she thinks and she stays quiet.

The baby is like calves, like puppies, and even chickens. María Antonia is no longer round. Just slightly fat. "What's she called?" asks Belinda without touching the sleeping baby. "Camila," says the mother. "Why?" asks Belinda, as if names could be explained. "From a movie," says María Antonia. "A girl falls in love with a priest and him with her, and because that's a sin they both end up getting shot by firing squad." Guille and Belinda exchange a look. They have caught themselves another story.

When they have finished the house on the hill, they transform it into a house for the priest and Camila. The police come for them and right there, up against one of the walls of the house, they are shot. Camila is in a white dress, with a bunch of yellow lilies in her hand, her hair up and dotted with violet flowers. She is blindfolded with a bit of green cloth. They use another part of the same cloth to blindfold the priest, who is wearing his cassock. A longer black dress that used to belong to Belinda's grand-mother. They say their last words: "We have no regrets" and "I love you."

The shooting plays out in slow motion, as if the soldiers took turns instead of firing together, a stream of bullets that passes through the bodies many times making them dance against the wall of the house. They fall to the ground and, still blindfolded, they drag themselves over to one another. They take each other's hands. Guille purses her lips tight. Belinda never quite ends up dying. Guille lets out a giggle and Belinda catches it. "Don't laugh," she says. They both laugh, lying there on the ground, Guillermina belly up, Belinda on her side. There's nothing can make them laugh quite like death.

And one time they played at being dead. "What must it be like, being dead?" they'd wondered.

They went down the hill to where the ground is mud, bringing spades, and dug two holes the size of their bodies. They'd picked hydrangeas at the big house and surrounded their graves with them. Then they took some mud and smeared it over their faces with both hands. Placing a sheet into each of the two holes, as if they were beds, they lay down on them and wrapped themselves up.

Belinda was holding a little bunch of limp daisies and a prayer card of Saint Jerome. Guillermina crossed her arms over her chest, holding a plastic rosary.

They waited a while and the mud advanced of its own accord. There were no tides in that place that was neither sea nor lagoon but merely a swamp, yet still the mud advanced, as if it were hungry.

"How's your death?" asked Belinda. "Cold," replied Guille, "and a bit uncomfortable. The bugs are eating me, I think." "I'm ascending and I can't feel anything anymore." "Belinda, I'm sinking." "You are dust and to dust you will return," said Belinda solemnly, her eyes closed.

Guille felt like she was made of mud. Belinda saw herself as a saint. Saints are beautiful, she thought.

Then they lay in silence for a little while.

When they tired of being dead they ran to wash themselves in the bathtub that stands beside the shed and always fills with water. They both got in and they were boats.

That night Belinda's mother saw the dirt under her nails and told her to scrub herself with the brush. Belinda used the horse brush.

Nobody said a word to Guille and she sniffed her hands, in bed, and fell asleep remembering that afternoon's sweet death.

One Saturday morning Belinda's father tells his wife that they'd done the butchering only he didn't get anything. Belinda's mother says that was one strange cow, missing some parts, kind of incomplete.

Juan Arancibia chews the toothpick and says the problem cow was called Cáceres and that he is going to sort the guy's parts himself now.

When they sit down to lunch Belinda's mother says not to forget it's Cáceres who's in charge at the ranch these days. Juan Arancibia smiles. Juan Arancibia never smiles. Can't be good he's doing it now. Belinda says nothing. Nor does she mention this to Guille.

And nor does Guillermina say anything when on the Sunday after the asado, Jacinto, her eldest brother, who is now also a farmhand, tells their father: "And what's the word on Arancibia's breaking-in, how that's going?" Eusebio Cáceres pauses before replying.

"Kinda useless, that animal," he says at last, as he arranges the tobacco strands on the paper.

Jacinto laughs, draws a whip from the back of his belt and holds it out to his father, who, ignoring his son's joke, moistens the bit of paper, rolls it and sharpens the tips several times. He inhales deeply and swallows.

When he lets the smoke out it doesn't seem to come from his lungs but from much further away, from some deep corner of his soul.

"Put that whip away if you're not gonna use it," Jacinto's father chides him, and he obeys, no longer in the mood to make jokes.

Eusebio Cáceres takes another puff, like someone who is holding very still, searching in the quiet for the impulse to pounce.

Small towns like fights. Gossip swirls around them like bugs around light and shit.

The different versions were born at different points, they crossed with one another and fed one another, they tangled and some fell away. The only points on which they all coincided were the shots of gin, the exchanged glares and the fact that no two people have been at each other's throats in recent years quite so much as Arancibia and Cáceres.

And everyone knows what blood is like, the way that once it bursts out it starts asking for more, it summons, and a few minutes later, two men who only wanted to square up to each other now want to see each other's guts exposed to the air. Arancibia lost an eye and according to some his honor.

Cáceres, who was rougher and more resilient, was just about ready to bleed to death but, perhaps only to annoy Arancibia, to beat him somehow, he revived.

Somebody said something about lawyers and filing reports, but both men agreed that such things were for pussies.

Arancibia and his family moved out to the town, like a dog skulking away after a fight.

Cáceres didn't tell him to do it, nor would he have.

Arancibia left of his own accord.

Hand-to-hand fights between men are capable of resolving things without changing anything.

Cáceres continues to think Arancibia is uncooperative and Arancibia still believes he ought to have been put in charge and not Cáceres, but it is as if these same thoughts had managed somehow to fit together.

Though it's true, there is now a tacit agreement over territory: Cáceres on the ranch, Arancibia in the town.

Belinda cries as she carries things when they move, and as she arranges them in the new house that she hates.

"It's not a farm shack," her mother says proudly, and Belinda cries.

She is still crying when she goes to the local school, she cries as she copies things down from the blackboard and during recess and she comes back home crying where she helps, crying, to prepare dinner and wash the dishes.

But she cries as if she were breathing. Just a few sparkling lines, like snail tracks across a wall, running down her face. A continuous crying under the equally silent and continuous threat that if she tries to go back to the ranch they will move further away still. No Arancibia must ever break the agreement.

Two days later Guillermina appears, like a kind of miracle, like an unexpected moon, practically on the haunches of the horse being ridden by Carlos, María Antonia's husband, who is bringing merchandise to send to Buenos Aires.

Every three or four days, Guillermina manages to get into town. There's always somebody to take pity on her: she arrives one day in Hernández's Rastrojero pick-up, another day on horseback with Antonio, another day on a bike with one of the Polish twins.

And they play. They play just like before and they open up that space outside the world, or rather, that leaves the world outside, they make it look ridiculous, they show it up.

On the first day they play at having a belly, both of them, that round belly they saw on María Antonia. Each uses a ball and they put their hands underneath to hold it up, just like real pregnant women do. Belinda is going to have a baby girl, and Guillermina doesn't know, but the father is one of those veterinary products salesmen who sometimes come by the ranch in a car.

Guille has yearnings, Belinda nightmares. She dreams of trees pursuing her. Guillermina tells her to put a knife under her bed.

On another day they play at being women from the "Oasis," that house with the red lights that's on the main road and which everybody talks about either smiling or angrily.

"There are women there in their bras and panties," Belinda's mother told her when she asked. They also heard something about how those women make the men have a few drinks. They imagine the women with made-up eyes, covered in necklaces, bracelets, and large earrings. The men fight over them and the women watch, drinking Coca-Colas at the bar.

The third time, Guille arrives with marks on her arms. "It was your dad," says Belinda. "No," replies Guille, "Jacinto, who's a jerk." "Because you're coming into town," says Belinda. "No, because he's a jerk," Guille says again.

Then there are many days that go by without Guillermina. They start up in the morning like something that's waiting to be filled and they continue like that, open like the mouths of fledgling chicks, until the night falls on them as if splitting them apart, if it is even possible to split nothing.

"It'll be tomorrow," thinks Belinda, so as not to die.

When Guille does arrive, her feet are hurt. Her father has told Jacinto to make sure she doesn't go anymore but to do it without hitting her, and Jacinto hid her shoes, her flipflops, and everything that could protect her feet on the three kilometers separating the town from the ranch.

Belinda washes Guille's feet in the basin with warm water and salt. Then she puts her own shoes on them and laces them up.

On that day, they do not play at all. They watch a storm coming in from the south, dark and inevitable, and they hug one another silently.

Guille doesn't tell Belinda that her mom has gone.

Impossible to know if it was Cáceres's idea or the owners', but soon afterward he and his children moved to another of the Arriaga properties, in Corrientes.

The first letter from Guillermina arrived nearly a month later. "The horses swim here and there are different birds." She no longer goes to school and takes care of her youngest brother, Cece. The house has hammocks, but she doesn't use them: she only rocks Cece.

She has learned to dance the chamamé. "When you come I'll teach you," Guille writes. But Belinda won't go to Corrientes. She finishes school and señora Beatriz teaches her to sew. The first thing she makes is a patch for her father's eye.

Belinda adores fashion magazines, especially bridal ones. Every bride in town wants a dress made by her. Belinda goes to all the weddings, she's with the brides practically up to the altar, arranging their train, their ruffles, their posture, their hair, and flowers.

When anybody asks why Belinda, who is so good and such a hard worker, has not married, she says weddings are work for her and she doesn't like bringing her work home.

The letters from Guillermina arrive three or four times a year.

Life can be measured out in those letters: 126 so far.

Belinda knows them almost by heart.

The rounded hand of the early letters moves her. The middle ones were letters that were constantly interrupted, and then, once some errand had been attended to, resumed.

Belinda imagines Guillermina's children. She has the photographs, but they are not enough. She imagines their voices, their games, everything that is missing from the photographs but so important. She looks at those photos over and over, she puts on her glasses, brings them close to her face, turns on the bedroom light and looks at them again.

"Your children are beautiful," she writes slowly a little while later.

Both women's parents have been dead for some time. Belinda does occasionally wonder why it is, then, that they are not together like before.

"Sometimes," she writes in block letters, "I remember the past."

She folds her letter, puts it in the envelope.

Guille replies that she can't look at her children without thinking of when they themselves used to play. That sometimes when she's scared of dying, she thinks it will be like lying in the mud of the lower ground.

"What joins you is separation." That is what Belinda's mother had said when she learned of the letters.

The last envelope has handwriting Belinda does not recognize.

"I am Guillermina Cáceres's daughter," she introduces herself.

"My mom died of Chagas." Then she says something about friendship and other things Belinda can't read because everything has clouded over. "Belinda Galván," she signs.

Suddenly there's nothing that doesn't hurt: her chest, her throat, her breath.

Belinda walks the road, carrying the pain along with her. She makes her way over to the ranch to find some hydrangeas.

When she reaches the swamp, she lies down on the earth and calls out to Guillermina over and over. But the silence closes in and the wind blows on.

After a while, and with some effort, she gets back up.

Without brushing herself down, she walks across the field. It looks like a sheet filled with stories, that field.

It also looks as though the hill has moved further away.

She tries to find the place and she does, despite there being nothing left now of the house. All the remains of The Secret are a part of the hill now, part of the earth and the trees.

Belinda sits down between two acacias. Night falls slowly.

The bird that is just barely singing does seem to be the same one as before.

RICE

Today is Thursday and on Thursdays we have lunch together.

We talk a lot, or what for us is a lot. Neither one of us is a person you would consider chatty.

Sometimes we even have lunch in silence. A silence that's comfortable, light as the air it's made of, in which the taste of what we eat can express itself all the better.

Other times when we talk the words make up little mounds that slowly turn into mountains. In between, we slip into long silences: valleys in which we think as if walking.

We choose a restaurant that's in an old house in San Telmo. It has a central courtyard, a square with its own sky, clouds that are never the same.

The conversation with my father moves at a tranquil pace.

Suddenly, in the middle of a sentence, he says "…was cleaning rice…" and he brings his hands together, making a ring with his fingers, and moves them as if striking something against the edge of the table. The suddenness of what happens is not in his saying these words but my realizing I don't know how you clean rice. The suddenness is my realizing there are a lot of things about him I know like this, not knowing them but somehow sensing them.

I know that my father's hands must be holding a sheaf of something I cannot see. I search my memory for the rice fields I saw in Japan and imagine the sheaf must be those kinds of green reeds.

I deduce clumsily that the rice must be stuck to the plants, and when they are shaken, it must fall. Like tiny fruits or seeds.

Seeing my father's movement, I can gain access to the past, to Japan or to my father's history, which is my own. Like the impressionists, not looking for the details but for the light, just the way I know the trees on the sidewalk outside my house, not knowing their names and yet unable to imagine my house without them.

That is how I talk to my dad: secure and groping blindly.

He says for example that this country is "only two hundred years old," it's a country that's "still just a child," he says, and alongside that small child I see an aged Japan, the skin on its hands covering and uncovering the shape of the bones.

If he grabs his head when he says they were running through the tea fields, I know there are planes flying over that I cannot see and they're dropping bombs.

We look at the menu and choose some dishes to share. My father never got used to just having one dish. It was my mom who got used to preparing several dishes for each meal.

Later we talk about books. He's reading *Mozart*, by Kolb, and he takes it with him wherever he goes. My father always has a book and a dictionary with him.

As someone who was born and raised in Argentina, I can't be bothered to look words up in the dictionary, I didn't even when I was just a girl. Not him. The Spanish of my Japanese father is vaster and more correct than mine.

He tells me his doctor sent him for some tests and while he was waiting he read a few pages.

"What tests?" I ask. "A biopsy," he replies. I'm afraid. I feel what is lurking in the shadows, and a certainty like the one that tells us night will follow day, a kind of vertigo. Everything I've never asked over the years comes back to me. Every question comes back and it brings others. I want to know why my father chose this country, this country in its infancy. I want to know what it was like on the day he learned that the war had started, what each of the days that followed were like until the day he reached this place. I want to know what his toys were like and his clothes, what it was like going to school during the war, what the port of Buenos Aires was like in the sixties, if he wrote letters to my grandmother, what they said. I want to know the colors, the words, the smell of the food, the houses where he lived. He told me once that when he arrived, he wouldn't get into the bathtub but washed outside of it and only immersed himself in the water when he was clean, because that is how they do it in Japan. I want him to tell me more things like these. Many of them. All of them. I want him to recount each day, so that time does not blow it away from us. Perhaps to write it down: leave it captured in ink on paper forever. Where to start? Where do the questions start? Which one comes first?

I look inside, as if running lost through this valley of silence that has opened up suddenly between the words. Getting lost somewhere so vast is a kind of confinement.

When I stop searching, I see the question right in front of me as if it were waiting for me. I look at my father and speak my question.

He smiles, takes a piece of paper from between the pages of his book and pulls a black pencil from his jacket pocket. He draws lines very close together, some parallel and others crossing. Then another, this one perpendicular and wavy, which cuts across them close to one end. These are the rice plants in water. Then he makes some very small circles on the tips: the grains. He tells me they gradually fill up and he draws these lines once again but rather than straight they are now curved at the tops: the plants when the rice ripens. "The fuller one is, the more polite, the more humble," he says. "You bend like the rice plant with the weight of the grains." Then he holds out his hands and arms and moves them parallel to the floor. "They would put big pieces of cloth over the field," he says. I imagine them white, rippling slightly, the way water moves when it's calm.

He once again positions his hands as if he were gripping a small bundle and he shakes it like he did before, against the edge of the table. Now I can see them clearly, I can almost touch them, the grains of rice falling loose.

THE NAMES

There are many things that have no name. Certain moments in the day, like the russet color between a bright evening and nightfall, and certain gestures, certain rhythms, some parts of the body, some colors like the greens that are neither sea nor moss.

But what has no name does still exist.

We stopped naming my brother the day he left the house, when I was eight years old. And as if that same blow had swept them along with him to oblivion, some of his things lost their names as well. One part of the house, an area of the river where he used to swim, his friends, what he liked, what he used to do. All of this likewise stopped being spoken.

And even the law that determined the erasing of all of these names was imposed without being spoken, the way fog imposes itself, or cold.

My mother could forget anything at any moment, or remain silent for whole days.

I don't know a lot about her and I don't even know if she found it hard to stop naming my brother. She seemed constantly preoccupied with something happening somewhere else, somewhere very far away.

Sandra and I didn't talk much either. But our silence was slightly different from my mother's.

I know that the Inuit, because they see so much snow, can differentiate and name ten types of white. I learned to differentiate between many different types of silence, but, unlike the Inuit, I did not name them.

Once, while Sandra and I were watching television, I asked her what had happened that day. "Why'd he go?" I said. "'Cause Dad hit him," she replied without looking at me and then she said as if she'd already told the same story many times over: "Mom and I were outside. Dad arrived and said he was tired and he was going to rest a bit. When we went inside, Dad was sitting there and he was laid out on the floor, with his arm bent at an impossible angle." I was trying to hurry, to ask what was most important.

I knew Sandra: I was sure she wouldn't tell me much more. "Had Dad hit him before?" "That time he stole from the Mejías place." Sandra was watching a woman make a table mat out of ice-lolly sticks. "Did he leave that same day?" "Yeah," said Sandra. "Mom cried all night." "And what about me—did I cry?" "No, not you," said Sandra before getting to her feet and turning off the TV.

The distance between me and my sister was not only a matter of years (she had seven on me), nor was it anything that might possibly be breached: it was solid. And asymmetrical, like those panes of glass that are mirrors on one side: I could see her, she could not see me.

We girls did, however, share a secret. At home, Sandra was always on the verge of or in the middle of an enormous rage, biting her lip, arms crossed, puffing, or throwing herself into an armchair as if she wanted to bomb it with her body.

But at school, I had seen her: Sandra laughed, she was more talkative, and she moved as if she were softer and lighter. At home, I alone knew about that other Sandra.

Or maybe we were all different out of the house.

When she finished school, Sandra married an old man.

On the day of the party the Sandra who laughed gave her secret away and went out into the world, and in order to bring a kind of emphasis to herself, she invented a new gesture: throwing back her head, as if she wanted to fill the air with laughter.

The old man was called Don Julio, he had a lot of money and he talked less than my parents.

The tables were decorated with white flowers and ribbons. We had spent the whole morning making the arrangements: I would count out three spikenards, four roses, a whole heap of ferns and a bow, and my mom would make a different arrangement each time.

My mom was especially good at that sort of thing, getting objects to respond to her in some way.

At the party the conversations, shouts, and laughter were bubbling at every table, but there was one where three people sat in silence: they were my dad, who just ate with his eyes fixed on his dish, Don Julio, who chewed slowly with his eyes on Sandra, and my mom who only ever moved to pour them some wine.

It was the contrast with those other tables that exposed the quiet of that one. Other people. Always others showing difference, making that difference finally fall upon us like an accent.

Other people with their eyes pointing like fingers, and their murmuring like flies that resist being shooed away.

Other people were saying that my brother had done something to me and that's why my dad had hit him. Other people always knew something, but nothing you could ever ask.

Soon Sandra changed again: she was blonde and she came to visit us in a black car.

Once she stayed with us for several days. She cried just sitting there on the bed and not bothering to cover her face, as if the tears were falling from her eyes without her noticing. She slept day and night.

I had put flowers on the tray Mom served her food on, but she didn't notice: she barely ate.

The dog had had puppies and I chose one with white gloves and boots, and on Sandra's last day I put it inside the black car, in a box with a T-shirt that no longer fit me.

I think it was my brother who'd brought that dog. Or had it been the other one, the male, that he'd brought? What remained of my brother in my memory were loose, blurry pieces. Making them fit together into a story would have been like trying to make a new dress out of tatters. But just as a shadow is shaped like whatever it's chained to, so forgetting only takes the shape of whatever it is covering. My forgetting was exactly the shape of my brother.

After he'd left, my dad hit doors, tables, the TV set, the chairs, the walls, as if he had blows leftover and needed to get them out. With time they dwindled, and at first this saddened me, like everything that comes to an end.

Not my mom: she stopped dragging her gaze along the ground and started to make it climb across things again, like a vine.

And as if spring or summer had arrived, with the days turning longer, everything was easier in the years that followed.

I moved to Buenos Aires to study geography, I'd visit Sandra once a week, and I got a job handling complaints at a telesales company.

The purchasers tended to get really furious and there was something about their fury that captured me as though I were being seduced. It wasn't the insults or the threats but the strength of their anger because a massager did not perform the functions it promised or a deep fryer hadn't lasted very long. I liked my job. The memory of my brother, or rather his forgetting, had been gradually left behind, as if recent events had been covering it over, the way you spade earth over the coffin of a dead man.

One night when we were watching a movie I asked Sandra what she'd done with the puppy I'd left in the car that time.

"What else was I going to do?" she said, not looking at me. "I threw it away."

In those days Sandra talked about killing Don Julio little by little: she would salt his food, tire him out, confuse him. But she was the one who looked tired. Don Julio, meanwhile, had been rejuvenated.

I lived with two cats, Simón and Odessa, and I taught at the Colegio Superior. There was always one student I didn't like. Though that does make it sound as if I liked the others…

No matter how many there were or what they were like, there was always one student who seemed to be the chosen one, and if I tried to feign indifference it only made matters worse.

When it was time for me to tell them their grades it was like they were suspended. Red roots would appear in their eyes, eyes that were fragile and moist as bubbles. Who doesn't like looking at bubbles? It was only a few drops of time, yet there was something nourishing in the intensity of those seconds.

By day I taught classes and by night I assembled jigsaws, with Odessa and Simón.

One December night the phone rang: "He's had a fall in the bath," said my mom. I imagined my dad, naked, disjointed, the shower still on, the water running over his empty body. The indifference of objects.

That same night I managed to complete an image of *Las Meninas* in 1,800 pieces. First I would classify the pieces, then I'd get familiar with them all and arrange them, just to feel the relief of placing the final one. Out of all the pieces, that was the only one that mattered, but how were you to recognize it in advance?

I looked at *Las Meninas* and discovered that behind the girls was a man I'd never seen before, leaving through a doorway.

I realized that I was now alone, or rather I realized that up until that moment I had not been. As if I hadn't known how to distinguish between solitude and its opposite, whatever that was.

My father was the only person I'd been able to talk to. He talked little and he asked questions that could be answered with a monosyllable, but if I had pulled on the thread of any of his words I could perhaps have unwound a conversation.

Not so with my mom. She had more words but fewer points. She had withdrawn to the world of objects: she always had something to tidy, to fix, to sew, to clean, to buy.

All women who have a house are concerned with such things, I know that now, but my mom abstained from any other kind of existence, and people and all their codes and customs disappeared for her. She was quite capable, then, of spending five hours in the supermarket, because prior to buying a product she would read the labels on every brand, do some calculations, and pause at each shelf for her own private conversation.

At my father's funeral she cried and I couldn't help wondering why. As if a part of me believed she hadn't loved him, or that she couldn't love anybody, as if it was possible to take care of someone without loving them.

I didn't recognize a lot of people. I allowed myself to be hugged while doing nothing, others did it all: surrounding me with their heavy arms, running their hands over my back, bringing their faces close to mine, all damp and shining and coarse.

One of the strangers took hold of my arms and said my name and that he'd seen my brother in the south, in Puerto Deseado, that my brother had worked with his son on a fishing boat.

When I told Sandra she said she knew already. Sandra was like that.

I couldn't possibly replace that phrase—"like that"—with any other. The next day I returned to Buenos Aires.

It was January and my apartment was like the sole survivor in a dead city. Odessa had fallen sick and the woman next door hadn't taken her to the vet. She was constantly drinking water and she didn't eat. "Kidney failure," the vet said. I did everything I could to make her final days good ones.

One morning when I woke up and saw her, curled at the foot of the bed as always, I knew I shouldn't touch her: she would be cold. Cold like my dad when I gave him a last kiss. The last and first. There was something in the way Odessa was sleeping that was definitive, that concealed no dreams.

What happened in the days following was what happens in such cases: Odessa's name floated all about the house, settling into her corner on the green armchair, searching for the little moving square of morning sun.

Sometimes I would say her name, in full or in part, when I arrived home, or when I heard a noise like the one she used to make with her nails on the living-room rug.

But then something strange happened: Simón started answering to Odessa's name, as if the only way of not missing her was to replace her, to transform himself into her.

It took me two days to make the decision, and finally I brought Simón to the Botanical Garden.

It was weird finding a place like that in the middle of the city, hidden away and abandoned yet at the same time so alive. Different species grew all tangled up with each other and there were so many greens that you didn't even notice the lack of other colors. The air was sweet, and right there, floating in it, there were butterflies. It had been years since I'd seen a butterfly. I was stirred by them, as if they had gotten inside of me.

Simón didn't want to come out of his plastic crate. Glued to the back as if heaped into a pile, raising his hands to defend himself, he made me sad. And that sadness confirmed my decision to return him to where he belonged in spite of the risk that he might not survive.

I don't know how they were related, the deaths of my father and Odessa and the idea of going to look for my brother, but two days later, I boarded a plane to Comodoro Rivadavia, the closest city to Puerto Deseado. The only way of getting to the port was to cross a part of the Patagonian desert from there.

It seemed appropriate that the thing I desired—the "Deseado" that gave the port its name—lay beyond a stretch of the hardest, the most hostile, the most arid land. But when I arrived at the longed-for town itself, I discovered it was merely another kind of hostility and hardness.

I took a hotel room from which I could see the pier where all the small boats docked. As if I knew which boat it was, and what my brother was like.

I spent my days walking and assembling jigsaws. You couldn't get hold of them in Deseado so I asked Sandra to mail me a few. I don't know whether it was a matter of space or of weight, but she just sent me the bags of loose pieces. I discovered, then, how much more interesting it was to decipher an image than to copy it from the lid of a box.

I believe there are some chess players who think through their moves more effectively if they aren't looking at the board. So I too walked the cliffs thinking about the pieces, their colors, shapes, and secret keys. The air smelled of the sea and in its own way that did seem good.

Without speaking his name, and without knowing that he'd decided to use my mother's family name, it wasn't easy to find my brother on the crew lists.

When I did track him down, I was told those boats didn't operate in the summer.

I decided to wait, and, as if planning to stay, I looked for work.

Having ruled out a few other options, I found two jobs that might keep me busy and earn me a little money: child-care at an oil company and a bar near the port.

The man who ran the bar just told me the schedule and the salary and clarified that if I wanted to do "a bit of work on the side" with any of the sailors, I'd need to pay a commission to "the establishment." That's what the man called the bar while he tucked his T-shirt into his trousers.

I never even showed up to my interview at the oil firm.

Among the women working at the bar there were quite young girls as well as prostitutes, and I felt more comfortable among them than I had in the teachers' room at school. All of them had two names: a real name and one they'd chosen for themselves that was always more beautiful than the first.

Some nights I thought about Simón. Would he have learned to hunt birds, to climb trees, to be who he truly was? I wrote Sandra a letter but never mailed it. It's hard to be silent in writing. My letter was incoherent. At least I could see that. There was only one paragraph in it I liked, and because of that I kept the letter. It was a paragraph about the desert.

The summer passed quickly, and autumn returned, which suited the Patagonian landscape particularly well.

I found that I was working at a bar at the end of the world waiting for somebody I didn't know and without understanding why. But after all, waiting is a place like any other: you can settle into it and make it your own place in the world.

Then, one September night, among a group of men, there was one who walked across the room as if he knew me. His face was drawn with straight lines, his skin hardened and there was a scar on his left arm. I wanted to say "Mario," but my lips seemed to be sealed shut, as if I couldn't get past the first letter of his name.

Suddenly I knew that for my whole life, my still lips had been repeating the first letter of that sleeping name. Sleeping in my still mouth.

"I'm Nati," was all I said. He didn't need to get any closer for me to smell him and to feel, affixed to his smell, my fear, and, as if I had climbed upon my fear to be borne back to that day, I was eight years old again.

That man approached me and my dad was no longer there to raise a hand and knock him off my body.

I think I shoved him and ran. I ran to the port and then to the road. My memories and the landscape rushed by me like a wind that sweeps across, cleaning everything it touches.

I was left smooth, a blank page, alone.

There are some answers that show up only to force us to ask the question, and when the two of them click into one another that tiny sound contains a key to all the peace in the world.

From that windy night, I was able to carry my name in a different way.

THREE
CHAIRS

There are three chairs on the porch making up a sort of triangle where a conversation must have taken place, one of those unending conversations on a summer evening. There may have been some yerba máte drunk too, because he did love bringing the chairs out onto the porch when the days got longer to drink some máte.

This ritual enabled a particular mood that was otherwise uncommon in him, this man who was always in a rush, always so practical. When drinking máte he waxed philosophical, almost poetic.

He would cup his hand over the old wooden gourd, yes, its thin silver bombilla sticking out, and without looking at us he would talk as if to himself or as if seeking to make his words float up into the air and not get carried off by the wind.

I used to like turning my chair around to listen to him, sitting with one leg on either side and my arms crossed over the back.

In these conversations I always need to be holding something: the back of the chair, a cushion, a cat, a glass.

He didn't need to rest on anything, his body was solid as a mountain. It imposed itself just as now his absence does upon these chairs that chat alone on the porch.

This absence repeats our last conversation like an echo. He had talked to me about the Serbs and the Bosnians and he told me the world had been at peace for fifty-six days of its history. It seemed a strange number. All wars are far off to me. He said that as long as somebody was at war, my peace would not be complete.

He always said these things that seemed to show me up, not so much to him as to myself.

I approach the chairs, as if approaching a group of people deep in conversation. With that subtle fear about interrupting at just the right moment, as if I were an instrument joining the melody that the band is already playing. Coming in without being noticed is a question of rhythm. But coming into silence is impossible.

And thus I remain for a few moments, a woman alone among the chairs. I don't dare sit down. That would be like sitting on top of somebody.

Without thinking and as on so many other occasions, doing what I imagine I ought to do, I rearrange the chairs. The three of them just like María used to position them, facing out, equidistant. Like a row in an imaginary theater that's watching the wind performing in the acacias.

Suddenly I see there's nothing human in this order, not so much as a ghost. Now I am even more alone.

Quickly I return the chairs to how they were, in imitation of that small warm circle. But the magic does not happen. It's just a new order that's as empty as the one before.

What's missing?

I lift one of the chairs a few centimeters off the floor and then lower it back into the same place, as if nailing it down.

What am I doing wrong? Why has my father disappeared, why is he no longer talking to me, sitting in these chairs, as he was until just moments ago?

FRAGMENTS OF A
CONVERSATION

She received me with her back to the door, jotting something down in a notebook.

"What is the great drama of your life?" was the first thing she said.

"There isn't one."

Now she looked up at me.

"All housemaids have a great drama to tell."

"Not me," I insisted.

"Maybe you're not really a housemaid then…"

"It's a job," I said. "I need the money."

"And you don't find that dramatic?"

I think I shrugged.

"Where were you born?"

"In the country."

"And you studied?"

"Yes."

"Got married, had kids?"

"No."

She went on looking at me.

"I do think there's something dramatic about your story."

"Depends on your parameters."

"You see?" she said, pointing at me now. "You use the word *parameter*!"

I had no idea where that word had come from. Not that word nor any other.

"Yeah," I said, "don't you, señora?"

"And what other difficult words do you know?"

"Difficult?"

"You're clever. You probably don't clean very well."

"I'm not clever."

"Seems to me you are."

"Well," I said, "I guess that depends who's measuring it."

"Parameters again…" she said.

"You use that word too, señora."

*

"Teresa."

"Yes, señora."

"Did you hear what Raquel said at our bridge game today?"

"I try not to listen."

"Quite right," she said, and I don't know if she was talking about good manners or about how foolish and rude her friends can be.

"Raquel was talking about how housemaids are always sneakily misappropriating things for themselves."

I said nothing.

She asked me what I thought about that misappropriating.

I said I didn't know who she was, this Miss Appropriate señora Raquel was referring to.

She laughed and said she was going to tell her friends that one.

Then she called me again and said that if I was Miss Appropriating, then she was Our Lady Of-Leisure, and she went on laughing.

*

Sometimes she'd call me over then not give me anything to do. She'd call me over and just talk nonsense. She seemed to have something to say. Or rather, she seemed to be waiting for me to say something.

One day she summoned me to her and said:

"Teresa, if I were to dismiss you—paying your severance and everything else you're entitled to, naturally—and you went to work over at Marita's, for example, seeing as she's on her own, and if she gave you not only weekends but also Wednesdays off, would you come visit me?"

I didn't know what the answer was, the right answer.

She told me I could get back to work. That the only thing that matters with some answers is how long it takes them to arrive.

*

"What do we need, Teresa?" she would say before going to the supermarket, and I'd make her a list.

When she forgot to take it with her, she would come back with any old stuff.

The one thing I never wrote down was yerba and it was the only thing she never forgot, even though she didn't drink máte herself.

*

"They're fucking wasted," she said when I asked her what had happened to the flowers.

She had started drinking and using bad language, too. I've never liked bad language. I changed the water in the vase.

"Teresa, come here, tell me the truth, aren't the roses more beautiful like this?"

"I dunno," I said, and she made me sit beside her on the sofa.

"You know, Teresa, somebody once said you need to look at a rose until your eyes pulverize."

Then we looked at the roses.

It was true, they did seem happy, but I didn't tell her this.

I denied it to the end.

The following day they were dead.

On the sofa she told me that señor Juan Carlos was going to leave her. We both knew that anything we discussed on the sofa was as if it had never been said.

The sofa was the place of what could not be said.

I would hit the cushions every day to plump them up, as if nobody had ever sat there.

*

"I don't know why you thought I asked you along," she said in the taxi back.

"For the company."

"In what sense?"

I said nothing but looked at her.

She insisted: "In any case, once you realized, I don't know why you didn't do what I told you."

"It didn't seem right."

"And since when is it your place to judge whether what I do is right or wrong?" she said, turning her body toward me.

"I'm not talking about you, señora, I'm talking about me."

"Telling me three crappy letters on a poster can't be bad."

"We were at the optician's, señora…"

"And the optician was out of the room, Teresa… You just had to tell me the letters before he came back."

I didn't answer.

*

"Teresa, I taught you to serve at table, to cook, to manage accounts, why can't you just learn this too?"

"Señora, I can't."

"Well, *I* learned, Teresa, didn't I? You just need to let out the clutch while you press down on the accelerator."

"Yes, señora, but you've also got to be looking at the gearstick, and watching the street, and looking in the mirrors…"

"But you get used to all that, Teresa. You look at everything without even realizing you're doing it."

"And what if I crash, señora? Everybody's got to do their thing. You don't know how to run the washing machine, I don't know how to drive the car…"

"Look, Teresa, if I needed to learn to run the washing machine I'd do it. If you couldn't see the buttons on the washing machine, or if it was dangerous, I would do it."

We went twice around the parking lot and came back.

She never would have learned to run the washing machine.

*

"Teresa, my aquamarine earrings are missing."

"The sky-blue ones?"

"Don't play stupid, Teresa."

I wasn't sure whether the aquamarines were the sky-blue ones.

She said she'd put them in her jewel box after Marianita's wedding and hadn't touched them since. She said I was "just another dumb black" even if sometimes I might seem different from all the others. She said she only didn't throw me out on the street 'cause she took pity on me, but that one day her pity would run out.

She was wearing the sky-blue earrings.

*

The señora was in my bedroom when I got back from the supermarket. She said it was horrible and that Marianita's bedroom had been unoccupied for more than ten years.

"Wouldn't you like it?"

"Señora Mariana's room is señora Mariana's room," I replied.

"Mariana has a room in her own house now, with Diego, and she won't ever be using this one again."

She wanted me to swap bedrooms. I'd have to sleep in the room next to hers. She would see me each time I went to the bathroom.

"I'll have to think about it," I said, and I remembered those answers that only matter for how long they take to arrive.

We never raised the subject again. Nor that of the earrings.

*

It was August fourteenth. That was the only reason. On August fourteenths, such things could happen.

I sat down on the sofa.

"Teresa!" she said when she saw me.

I said nothing, and she sat down and stayed there, sitting in silence as if she had just understood something.

"I told you a lie, señora," I said.

She said nothing.

"When I first came. You asked what the great drama of my life was."

"Me?" she said, bringing her hand to her chest the way she sometimes did.

"Yes, you, señora. I said there was nothing dramatic about my life. That was a lie," I said.

And then I told her.

The following day, August fourteenth had passed and silence floated over the couch as always.

I didn't know whether I'd been right or wrong to do it. Certainly I felt better. But sometimes you feel better after doing something bad.

We didn't talk about that again either.

Sometimes she seemed to know things without even realizing.

"We're alone," she said to me one day after Alfonso asked me to move in with him. "We're alone you and I, Teresa. We only have each other."

Alfonso was a building manager. We'd been seeing each other on weekends for two years. He treated me like a queen.

"Juan Carlos has gone. Mariana has gone. My friends are non-existent. Yours even less."

She went on talking. She'd been drinking.

Alfonso seemed to be telling her "no" inside my head. I wanted to tell him to keep quiet, not to hurt her, that this would pass, she was a good person.

But Alfonso didn't seem to care. He went on smiling inside my head.

*

On August fourteenth she brought me a gift. It was a little music box.

"It was my mother's," she said, and she gave it to me. I had seen it in the closet.

It was Monday and on that Saturday and Sunday I'd gone with Alfonso to the river. There were so many birds.

I'd almost forgotten what day it was. That had never happened to me before.

*

"Señora, I'm going, I'm going off to live with Alfonso. I'll be six blocks away. I can still come see you."

"Señora, I am fond of you, but Alfonso wants me to go live with him."

Only I never said these things to her.

Whenever I was about to say them, something else always came out of my mouth.

Sometimes when Alfonso called me on the phone I would get to thinking. I could almost see her saying: "How can you do such a thing to me?", either that or she'd do something terrible before saying, hand on her chest: "You made me do it, Teresa," as she had to señor Juan Carlos when she'd said all those things about him.

Then one Friday afternoon I sat down beside her on the sofa and looked at her.

She seemed to realize something. She didn't tell me to get up.

71

I remembered what she was like when I first saw her. She had dark hair, skin unblemished, eyes that seemed to be alight. They had gone out now. I thought about the yerba she used to bring home for me.

Then I got up and I don't know if she looked at me then or just went on watching TV.

That Monday I didn't come back.

THE BOOTS

Uphill she goes slower.

She lifts herself off the seat and pedals to go faster. She throws the whole weight of her body from side to side. She's going to be late.

She leaves the burnt-down Pesca Sur plant behind her. Eyes fixed on every one of the sixty black meters ahead.

It's like a thing that isn't there. What's missing always triggers questions, she thinks to herself. Yet they are left behind there, on the path next to the bicycle tracks.

A few days ago, in the middle of a filleters' protest, some people in hoods burned down seven processing plants.

Fortunately, before she arrives the path tips downhill. She feels the rough wind on her face.

She greets the guard at the door, then runs, taking off her coat and dragging it behind her into the locker-room. She drops the bag onto a bench. She takes off her clothes and tosses them on the floor, and in seconds she's ready. All decked out: trousers, jacket, cap, mask, latex gloves. Like a surgeon. She looks for some boots. There's only one pair. They're size 35 and she's a 38. She puts one foot in and then the other. She's wearing thick socks.

She runs over to the plant, swipes her card and the display shows she's fourteen minutes late. She grabs a crate and a knife and makes for the filleting table where Lidia is.

The fish has just been unloaded. One of them is flapping about. She takes a deep breath and inhales the scent. She loves the smell of the sea when the fish come in. It bothers her when she hears someone talking about a fishy smell as if it was the smell you get in a Buenos Aires fishmonger's. That ammonia smell that assaults the nostrils and the spirit. "That's not the smell of fish," she says sometimes, shyly. Fish smell of the sea. She wonders then whether we smell of the earth.

"What happened to you?" Lidia asks her. "My littlest's got the flu." "You leave her at your old lady's?" "Nah, the eldest stayed to look after her. The nine-year-old, she's got the teachers' strike." They talk side by side, without looking at each other and never stopping filleting. "Did Romero say anything?" she asks. "Why, 'cause you were late? What's he going to say… Anyway, more people came. The boats that were doing the prawns have gone back out for the hake now."

She's the fastest of the filleters, and, just like in a Western, being the fastest commands respect. She takes up a fish, slices the knife quickly down one side, then the other, yanks out the spine, pulls off the skin, cleans out the insides, tidies up the edges, and thinks about her daughter's cough. Her toes are curled as if in reverence. She runs the back of her free hand over her pocket and checks she has her phone. Her gaze sweeps over the other tables. It's true, there are more people here than in recent weeks. She sees Susana.

The women's eyes, over their masks, exchange a greeting. Natalia's there too, the girl who started only a couple months ago. Natalia used to work at a club where the sailors go, but something happened and she didn't want to go back. Natalia is slow at filleting but quick to learn.

She finishes the crate, hangs her number on it and takes it to the table. The pain in her feet is getting more intense. She walks on her heels. She sees that Granny Tata is next to the tunnel freezers. Tata is the oldest of the filleters, probably around seventy. From Corrientes, like her own parents. And like many of the crew on the plant's boats.

Her mom said that's simply what nature was like, that just as some animals migrate in search of a better climate, they had come to Patagonia chasing after work. But when she said she wanted to be a filleter, her mother had also said that she hoped for something different for her. Now she understands what her mother meant, but her house never lacks food on the table and the girls go to school. She can't bear it anymore, she wants to take off those boots and throw them away. In the next box of new fish that she picks up, there are several with bruising. There'll be a lot of waste.

The previous week, the box that Granny Tata was working on when she cut herself got full of blood and they had to throw it away. Could that be why they moved her to the tunnel freezers? She nudges Lidia with her elbow and asks. Lidia says that when Granny Tata arrived she wasn't feeling well and Romero said she could get on with putting the trays in the tunnels instead of filleting. "It's colder there, it'll make it worse, won't it?" she says, but Lidia has already walked away with a crate.

Her feet have gone to sleep inside the boots. It's true, Granny Tata isn't looking too good.

The new knives are really great, they slide through the flesh like they're cutting through air. Her eldest kid hasn't called, everything must be OK, she thinks. She finishes another crate and carries it over to the table. A meter away Granny Tata collapses, bringing down a pile of stainless-steel trays that make a noise like an explosion. Some people run over to help. She retrieves the trays and piles them back up.

The manager says he'd like somebody to accompany Granny Tata to the bathroom until the doctor arrives. She volunteers because she can't bear those boots anymore. No way she'll be able to stay standing for the three hours she has left.

Between a few of them, they manage to drag Granny Tata to the bathroom. They sit her up against the wall and her head lolls slightly to one side. The old woman is very pale.

She sits down beside Granny Tata with her legs outstretched, then catches sight of the four feet all perpendicular to the floor. Tata's boots are two centimeters longer.

Her own feet throb.

She crouches down. Granny Tata's eyes are shut and her mouth half open and it seems likely she won't wake up for a good while.

She sits on the floor and pulls off one impossible boot and then the other. Her feet almost burst free of their own accord and once out they expand as if stretching.

Her violet- and fuchsia-striped socks stand out against the surgical white of the plant bathroom. A human gesture that evaded any calculation.

She takes hold of the heel and toe of Granny's left boot and pulls. The boot slips off toward her, and she puts it on before removing the other.

She puts her foot all the way in, then wiggles her toes around inside to enjoy the space. Tata is like the tower of Pisa, slightly listing. It must be the lack of one of the boots, or having the other still on. She gives the opposite shoulder a little push, and Granny teeters then collapses.

She decides to finish the business with the boots before straightening Granny Tata back up. She takes the heel and the instep of the right boot and pulls. This one's rebellious, it's not like the other one. She pulls harder. Granny moves toward her but refuses to play along. She turns her back, kneeling, wedges her in place with her foot and pulls again. This time the boot does come off. She gets up, slips her other foot inside, and makes her toes dance.

Granny Tata has lost her cap and her white hair is disheveled and it tumbles over her face. Her body is on the floor, with her head almost at a right angle to the wall.

Slipping her hands under Granny Tata's armpits, she sits her back up. Inadvertently her fingers touch her face and they feel cold. The old woman is icy.

She ought to put the small boots on her.

She looks at Granny Tata's feet, a nail poking out through a hole in one sock.

Although she tries to put the first boot on her, the thing jams on the old woman's motionless ankle.

She hears Romero approaching with somebody. A doctor and a stretcher-bearer. They take Granny Tata's pulse, look in her eyes, maneuver about a bit and finally stretcher her away. Nobody notices her whispered words: "I took her boots off of her so she'd be more comfortable."

She returns to the table and goes on filleting.

The following day they're told that Granny Tata died. She thinks about death: she wouldn't want it to get her while she was working. Nor in hospital. And also not at home. No, let it be in the processing plant, she corrects herself mentally. That's what she is. The rest comes later, a long way off.

She thinks about the boots. "Did she die or was she dead already?" she asks. "What's it matter what exact moment it happened?" says Lidia, running a handkerchief over her red nose and swollen eyes.

On that day some of the women don't stop talking, as if wanting to expel something from inside themselves. She and Lidia work their whole shift in silence.

When she leaves, she doesn't get onto her bicycle, she wheels it along, leading it by the handlebars.

She jogs over to Lidia and says: "I want to tell you something." Lidia looks at her. "I swapped Granny's boots in the bathroom. Mine were too small and they were killing me." Lidia looks at her and bursts out laughing. "Don't tell me you think that's how she died?" Lidia's laughter is contagious.

They walk together uphill to Lidia's house. "I want to tell you something too—come in and have a few mátes."

Lidia pours the water, sticks the bombilla into the gourd, and leaves it on the table. "Be right back," she says.

Lidia returns holding something black, which she tosses onto the table. "I was there," she says, "the day of the fires."

She picks up what Lidia has brought her. A balaclava.

Her face, like the desert, never changes much. But inside her there's a series of images that parade past like corpses: an overturned forklift, twisted iron, trampled fish, black hoods, and sticks.

She tells Lidia they'll do the mátes some other time, and gets onto her bike. She wants to go home. She stands up on the pedals to go faster. She throws the weight of her body and of her sadness from side to side.

The way home is downhill.

THE PIT

Sato the soldier receives an order from Captain Takeda, who has received an order directly from General Imagawa.

Sato the soldier is to dig a pit in the place indicated to him by Captain Takeda per the higher order from General Imagawa.

The fact that the order has come down from such a height directly to Captain Takeda without passing through any of the intermediate echelons in the hierarchy serves to armor it, makes it impervious to any questioning, to any doubts or any movement of ideas.

The order is a perfect block that is passed from hand to hand.

It's an honor that it has passed from General Imagawa's hands directly to Captain Takeda's, and Sato the soldier receives the block and the honor of holding it.

He is led to the assigned place and handed some basic survival equipment: weapons, tools, provisions, and a new metal spade with a wooden handle.

It is rare to see an impeccable item in a war. In the two years Sato the soldier has been in the army, he has never received an unused item before.

Captain Takeda stands at a spot as though it were marked with a red X.

He turns his sharp eyes on Sato the soldier and points at the red X that the soldier is beginning to see.

The captain says: "Dig here until further orders."

To somebody from another culture, the captain's forcefulness and his serious tone might sound fraught with annoyance or rage.

"Yes," says Sato the soldier from his belly, looking straight ahead.

Orders are received without looking at the person giving them, which allows these orders to enter and mingle with what one is.

The soldier remains in this position while Captain Takeda and the accompanying group withdraw. He feels them moving away, even without looking at them, without looking at anything but the posture of his own body.

Once alone, he looks at the spot indicated, picks up the spade, raises it, and allows it to drop down hard. He rests his foot on the edge to bury it deep, raises up the earth, and tosses it aside. He is struck by the color of the earth. It's redder than the earth in Japan.

He lifts the spade once more, and sinks it back in.

Then he repeats the movement.

He repeats it until he can feel the muscles of his arms and his back.

Still he goes on repeating it.

Then he stops. The mountain of earth looks bigger than the pit.

How long has it been? The duration of his tiredness. He looks around him. He finds the water, drinks slowly.

He runs the back of his hand over his forehead, then decides to arrange the things, to set up a base, do a roll call of all the gear so he knows what he has to rely on.

There are eight large bundles, occupying more space than all of Sato the soldier's belongings before the war.

He must find a place to set up camp. He looks all around.

To one side, a sort of plain: his vision expands and unfurls. To the other, a forest that doesn't allow his vision to enter more than a few meters.

He chooses the forest, and goes in.

There's a change in temperature, in the scent of the air, the light, the noises, in what can be seen, and what can be felt. From the forest the plain feels like an outside. You go out to the plain, come into the forest.

He walks the first few meters with his eyes sweeping from side to side, fanning across the ground.

He ought to pitch camp at a distance from which he can see the pit. When not digging it, he ought to guard it. He chooses an area next to a tree whose tentacle-like roots pass in and out of the earth, and where a fallen trunk offers the idea of a shelter amid all that verticality.

Only the idea.

Sato the soldier clears the stones, branches, and leaves from the ground until he can see the earth.

A square of clear earth. The fact of its being a square is significant only in its evocation of the shape of a house or a room.

He arranges the bundles into a kind of barricade, and decides to do the rest later.

He doesn't know when Captain Takeda is coming back and he has no time to waste.

Returning to the pit, he drinks a little more water and resumes his task.

As a boy he once needed to dig a pit. He recalls doing it with his hands and with the help of a stick. There was something he needed to bury. He can't remember what. He does remember having scratched the ground hard, felt the earth under his nails. His fingers stumbled upon stones that hurt but didn't stop them. He remembers the strength with which he held something in his hands. He remembers having buried it forever.

The earth is no longer quite so red, it's darkening now as the pit proceeds toward its proper depth.

The pit stretches out like a stain of nothing on the ground; Sato the soldier needs to move around it in order to continue digging.

He feels his tiredness but pays it no heed. The tiredness does not insist and, like the pit, it grows silently.

Sato the soldier notices that the light has been changing and the sun is hiding on the far side of the forest, from where he can still see a few red rays.

He searches in his pocket for his watch. It's the time when, if he were in town, he would have his dinner.

In war there are no schedules, at least not those of normal people outside of it. Some other schedules do exist which must be followed to the letter, but those are not determined by common soldiers, not even by captains.

Sato the soldier thinks that in the absence of precise

orders for how to carry out his task, he ought to do it in as organized and responsible a way as possible.

Judging by the supply of provisions, he is to dig for several days. That being the case, it isn't advisable to keep digging on the first day till he has exhausted all the strength of his muscles.

He decides to organize his shelter.

This island that doesn't appear on the maps hasn't yet been taken by the Japanese nor by the enemy.

If his mission had been part of an advance on enemy territory, they would have told him. He assumes that he is in a Japanese area or at least a neutral one.

In any case, in war one cannot count on anything with certainty, so he should make his shelter as safe as possible.

Around him he sees only trees, earth, trees, trees.

He decides to dig a small trench to protect himself when lying at ground level, in a firing position. He looks at the spade and is grateful to have it.

He starts digging and, before he's done, the night falls, with its owls, its frogs, its crickets.

They invade the soldier's solitude and as if he were waking up to something, he notices the tiredness inhabiting him.

He covers the ground with leaves, rearranges the bundles about him, takes one portion from his food rations and the canteen and sits.

The tiredness is like a heavy liquid flowing slowly between his bones.

He looks at the food and wonders what it could be made of. He remembers the food his mother used to make.

The way it smelled. He thinks about the smells from that kitchen and tries to inhale them. He almost manages it but falls asleep first, sitting in the trench. He dreams about his kitchen back home, in his town. He dreams of the smells and colors from before the war. The noises, gentle as oxen or running water.

When he wakes in the middle of the night it's almost as if he hasn't woken at all: he hears the noise of the water he'd been dreaming about.

He recognizes the forest, remembers the pit, looks unseeing at the floor, sharpening his hearing to catch the noise of the water. It's coming from the dark of the forest.

If he is going to enter some place he does not know, better to do it at night. If there are enemies, they'll be asleep or at least off their guard.

He follows the voice of the water calling to him, makes a mental note of the position of his shelter, and advances into the trees.

A stream of silvery water. A gash cutting through the forest and the moon floating white as a freshly made rice ball. The soldier crouches down, puts his fingers in the water. He cups his hands. Gently, he drinks.

Something settles. The soldier is doubtful about the war.

He returns to his trench and sleeps. When he wakes, he runs back to the stream to see whether it exists.

He washes. Drinks. Gives thanks.

Then he takes a portion of food and digs all morning, pausing occasionally. The depth of the pit comes up to Sato the soldier's belly.

He rests his hands on the edge, tenses, and jumps till his arms are locked straight, then hooks up one leg and gets out.

He looks down and is surprised. He remembers the red X. He doesn't know if he ought to go on digging downward or expand outward. Tilting his head to the left, he places a thumb on one side of his chin while two fingers crawl along the opposite cheek.

"I'm a fool," he thinks. "If they didn't tell me, it's because I'm supposed to know." He gets annoyed.

"Think, think," he tells himself, closing his hand now. A fist of annoyance.

He crouches down, one hand on the other, elbows on his knees.

In his mind he draws a picture of the island, how they'd gotten here, the route they took to this point between the forest and the plain, far from the sea. He realizes he's in the center. Perhaps a breakthrough point. One solitary point.

It's not the place for a military clash or he wouldn't be all alone. Perhaps reinforcements are on their way.

The night had been a quiet one. There are no other forces nearby, nor raids, nor villages. If the pit was for burying something specific, he'd have been given the dimensions.

The ideas come and go and bewilder him. Threads that cross over one another entangling him completely. "Fool," he says again, when he reaches a knot. Fool, fool.

"Dig here until further orders," Captain Takeda says again in Sato's head. The soldier takes a mental look at him.

He tries to find, hidden in those five words, some sort of key. Dig here until further orders. There will be further orders: this is a part of something. Just a part. Perhaps there are other soldiers doing the same thing at other points of the island.

A ditch, that's it. He must be digging a large, deep ditch.

A part of one. To divide up the island and prevent advances.

The plan for building walls hadn't worked too well on other islands in the archipelago. He's heard something about that.

If the enemy wanted to build bridges, they would destroy them at once. But with the walls, the opposite had happened: it was the enemy who'd torn them down before they even knew about it. Being able to see the enemy as they're advancing is important. Seeing is knowing. Knowing is mastering.

Yes, the pit must be part of a large, deep ditch running along the border between the forest and the plain.

Without realizing it, he has taken up his spade again and he is digging.

A part of something. The spade goes into the earth. He is always part of something. He tilts it, loosening the earth. He is a part. The spade comes up filled with earth. Being a part is also being the whole. He tips the spade onto the mound on one side. Part. Whole. Earth mixes with earth.

Sato the soldier is sweating. He takes off his shirt, wipes it across his forehead, and throws it onto his bag.

He drinks from the canteen, his face upturned. A ray of sunlight pins his eyes and explodes. Blinded by light, he is thirsty and hungry.

He looks at the pit and is amazed. That's what he feels

whenever he sees how much he has dug. He can't dig and look at the pit at the same time. You can't search for a result if you're looking at it. Searching and finding. That's how he feels when he looks at the pit: as if he's found it. Such a big pit. Now, he feels, he may have his lunch.

He goes into the forest as though entering his home, sits in the shelter as if at a laid table, and eats. The food puzzles him. It's like something that is not. It isn't tasty, but nor is it unpleasant. He feels nothing as he eats it. It's just something that consumes his hunger.

He opens the boxes: they're all alike. Daily allocations of two big meals and a small one, tied into bundles of seven, in boxes of five bundles. Four boxes. That's equivalent to four months.

The water would never last that long: they must have known the stream was nearby.

Nobody can dig a hole downward for four months.

It's a ditch. Of course.

His idea asserts itself now.

Something, he feels, slots into place. Him and the order. Him and the world. Both are round, they have teeth and they turn, the tooth of one slotting between two teeth of the other. Gears.

He finishes the ration and still feels hungry. He drinks more water.

That afternoon the spade rises, cuts through the air, falls, loads up, rises, empties out in mechanical motion. Machines do not make mistakes, do not get tired. Sato the soldier is a machine for digging.

In the clear sky there is one single smudge: a cloud. It moves along slowly, neither pausing nor hurrying, an even journey as though sliding across ice. One single cloud. Lost from its herd.

Sato the soldier digs and sometimes a memory passes by, neither pausing nor hurrying, as though simply gliding. He just looks at it. A passing cloud.

His childhood geta. He remembers his skinny feet, fans made of bird bones. He remembers them on the earth, in the rice fields, on the mountain, in the mud. His mother hunched over doing the washing. There was something about that posture that saddened him. Those shoulders curved forward, as if they needed to protect what was beating within. A body shaped like a cage.

He remembers his feet. He must have spent a lot of time looking down. He must have had the same posture as his mother.

Then he'd gradually straightened up like a plant seeking the sun, his shoulders widened a little and drew back, his thin chest came forward.

He digs without even noticing, and without even noticing he tires. Evening falls, pink and gold, and it embraces him.

He eats his rations outside the shelter, on the plain, staring out at nothing. Tasting nothing. The nothing brings him no pain, no fear.

Since the war began, the soldier has not had the chance to notice how bland the rations are. Nor has he been able to stop just because tiredness has been weighing on him.

He hasn't been able to look at the sky unless searching for enemy planes as he does so.

Tonight he sleeps without a gun at his side, he lies down and lets his body spread out when he dreams.

The next day he decides to keep count of the days, to track how much he's digging each day, so that when his superiors return he will be able to report back precisely and correctly.

On the fallen trunk there are three marks.

He recalls what he felt the previous day, his disdain for the taste of the food.

How stupid to think that the war doesn't exist just because from this vantage point he cannot see it. How stupid to think himself on the fringes of a war, being a soldier. He ought to repeat over and over to his foolish head that the war exists whether or not he sees it, and that he is a soldier, even if occasionally he enjoys privileges like being far from the front, or on such rich land, and having new items and everything he needs.

He ought to repeat this to himself daily so as not to fall into a trap that might put him genuinely at risk.

When he goes out to the plain, he sees a flock of clouds advancing, scattered.

Perhaps it'll rain. The rains on this archipelago last days. With his thumb on one side of his chin, his index and middle fingers run down the opposite cheek. It scratches. He shaves.

Then he opens up the bundle containing two thick canvas sheets. He'll use one for the shelter and the other for the pit. He can't stop digging just because of the rain, but nor can he get sick: that would come to the same thing.

He looks for sticks to make props. He takes up the axe.

In the forest he feels the crunching of the leaves differently now, softer.

The scent on the air is different, too. Humid, he thinks.

He finds some tree trunks and strips them with the axe. He first makes a cross to support each square of canvas and keep it in tension, like a kite. He knots the four corners and ties them with cords to the points of the cross, tightly. Then he ties these points to the props already buried around the shelter and on one side of the pit.

It's a luxury to have these small houses. In the Japanese army only the officers have tents. The mere thought makes Sato the soldier feel like he might be at fault.

He remembers that it is also his duty not to get sick. This dispels his sense of being at fault and the soldier takes ownership of the improvised canvas roofs.

As if it had been waiting for him, the rain begins to fall as soon as he has finished the job.

The rain keeps him company. He digs under the roof that is next to the pit. As if it were a small pit that was soon to join the mother pit.

The rain doesn't stop all afternoon. Nor does the soldier. When he left his town to join the army, it was raining. He remembers his mother's sad eyes.

He digs harder. From this position he won't be able to write to her. Even if he did, he might not be able to tell her about the ditch. He'd just tell her he's fine and that he'll be home as soon as the war is over. He remembers his mother's hands like two interlinked turtles. Turtles that are ancient, and good, and tired.

That night he dreams he's a boy again and his mother's hands are white and smooth. As if they were made of snow. And scented like summer nights. His mother's hands take flight of their own accord and escape. His maimed mother is holding him in her arms.

He wakes up scratching his face. He touches his cheeks, his neck, his arms and feels the bites. Tiny little burning volcanos.

The coolness of the stream gives him a bit of relief that passes over his skin as fast as the water.

He shouldn't scratch, he knows this. He doesn't scratch all day long and that night he drops down exhausted.

He improvises a kind of mask using a piece of medical gauze. He dreams of nothing.

The days that follow resemble one another just as each of the minutes resembles the others, just as each spadeful does too. The only difference is in the results: in the pit, in the muscles in his back, the food from the boxes.

The pit is no longer egg-shaped. It is a grub that has been born between the forest and the plain. On rainy days the bottom fills with water: the soldier doesn't dig down into the pit but expands its edges as if the grub were stretching.

He wears his mask to avoid getting bitten and he has discovered that the smell of one plant keeps the insects away. He opens up the fleshy leaves with his knife and rubs them over his body.

This new war that surrounds him in silence allows him to take note of the plants where previously he saw only forest or jungle. Where previously he saw only one, he now sees thousands, as if he has understood something.

His sense of smell has awoken. That's how the soldier feels. As if up till now it had slept, leaving his sight to do all the work.

With his sense of smell awakened, his sight and hearing have perked up too: he sees things he previously hadn't seen, he can make out sounds as if seeing them. As if he has discovered new weapons.

Something has shifted itself from inside out, from the center of the soldier to his surroundings. What is inside so resembles what is outside as to erase the boundaries. That line between the two is the actual outline of the soldier, who is turning into the forest and the plain and this black pit like a mouth filled with hunger.

With the soldier now become forest and plain, the war feels far away. His little town does too. And himself, the boy he was before the war.

When he sees that he is forgetting what he is and where he is, he reminds himself of it: he is a soldier, and he is at war. His mission is to dig a pit until further orders.

The grub pit has stretched out southward and northward, and its body made of lack has sunk into the earth: it comes up to the soldier's chest.

He has constructed a small staircase. On each side of the pit, there is a high border of earth.

The soldier can see the enemy tumbling into it, getting injured trying to cross over to this side of the earth. Because war splits the earth in two, like an apple, a walnut, a pear. Sato the soldier digs the crack that splits the earth. A part that is tiny in scale but vast in significance. What's the point of a dike if it has a hole in it, what's the point of a ditch if it doesn't separate the whole thing? The soldier digs, like an ant biting into a watermelon, a black dot smaller than a seed.

The soldier is tiny, like the tip of an arrow. Sato the soldier digs like a dagger in the earth.

The soldier's time is counted in identical spadefuls. He decides to stop marking off the days on the tree trunk.

There's no point to those marks: he isn't waiting for any particular date. The row of spider legs isn't headed anywhere. His superiors might come to fetch him at any point, today when the sun sets, or perhaps tomorrow when he wakes up again or perhaps in a month or two or a year.

When he reports back it will not be day by day, but one day repeated many times: a day in which he dug and then at night watched over the pit.

Or simply he will report having done as he was ordered.

Days are not people, each with their own clothes, whether poor or luxurious, their hands white or tanned, the looks in their eyes. Days are soldiers.

Drawing up the days on a tree trunk is like marking distances in water.

The soldier's time is the sea in which he swims: it is what sustains him and in which he might sink if his arms stop their strokes. The soldier's time is liquid, and is not measured with marks. The measure of time and of the soldier is the pit that progresses spadeful by spadeful.

In this liquid time the soldier's first attempt at swimming is something like a struggle. Then a dance. Finally, scales break out on the soldier's body: he has adapted.

On one of these unmarked days, the soldier again regrets the lack of any taste in his rations and almost at that same moment he sees a bird, a large one.

He constructs a trap, a kind of cage made of branches, and puts his ration inside as bait. He's prepared to lose a portion in exchange for hunting something that more closely resembles the food from before the war.

He rests the cage on a branch and ties the branch to a piece of string that he holds, hiding quiet and still.

His dinner falls into the trap.

Lighting a fire to cook it is a big risk: if there are enemy troops nearby, they will see the smoke, they will capture him, and the planned ditch will fail completely.

But his superiors have left him three boxes of matches, so it is clear he must be authorized to use them. From these matches he deduces that the enemy is not nearby.

The next time he tries to hunt a bird, it's a kind of rodent that walks into the trap, which is harder to cook but tastier.

Before eating, the soldier always gives thanks for his food.

Just like when he is seduced by the landscape, when the food is good the soldier keeps repeating to himself that he is at war as if tapping himself on the head. The war disguises itself as pleasures so as to trick him.

When he has only thirty servings of his rations left, he decides to do without them, to hold them back in reserve.

From the time that has passed he deduces that his superiors trusted that he would find subsistence in that place.

Or something unexpected has meant they haven't been able to return in time.

Everything is unexpected in a war. He should be prepared.

Nothing should surprise a soldier.

He walks turning on his axis, always. So as not to offer up his back as a target, so that no one might approach without his seeing them first.

His walk is not a line but a spiral, the longest distance between two points, the safest.

He has never felt any concrete threat that could be coming from the enemy. Voices, smoke, the noise of bullets or bombing.

This life sometimes resembles a drowsiness. The same kind that makes birds or rodents fall into traps.

The rainy days return, riding upon fat clouds like poorly sketched horses.

The soldier wonders if this will be a rainy season like the last one or an isolated shower. He prepares the canvas roof.

He digs all day beneath the roof. He reaches the edge of his dry shelter: he can't dig anymore.

He sits down on the bottom. The spade at his side, he rests. Threads of water come down from the walls and fall like festoons: there are holes in the roof.

Whenever he stops digging the soldier feels his tiredness.

He stretches out one leg, rests an arm on the other knee. His hand hangs limply, wet. A drop trickles down his index finger. An ever-deepening curve that comes loose and leaps to its death.

The soldier looks at many of them, all in a row. Soldiers of water.

Memories parade past and he does not look at these. But memories don't like to be ignored. Some of them, like clouds that do not rain, turn denser. Others change shape, dissipate, disappear.

He makes a mound out of the mud from the bottom of the pit. He looks at it until he sees a face. When he sees it, he sculpts it. When he recognizes it, he names it. He calls it Unno, like his best friend from childhood.

And from out of his mouth sprout names that begin to rename each thing.

The second name is a woman's and it falls on the spade: Sachiko.

He remembers Sachiko, his friend's sister. He remembers how she moved, her face, her walk as if floating.

Women are closer to nature, which is why they retain their mystery. Their motives are like the motives of the dew, of leaf fall, of waves.

The soldier looks at Sachiko the way you look at the moon.

Then other names burst from his mouth and fall on the bundles, the weapons, the plants.

Everything has a name except the pit. The pit cannot be named.

The soldier sculpts more faces in the mud and names them. The pit fills with faces that within the darkness keep the soldier company, smile at him, watch over him, ignore him, shout at him, invite him for a drink, tell him things, give him orders. Some voices are much louder than other voices. It is not the soldier who decides how loud each one is, it's the pit.

The soldier no longer hears them separately, rather they have become one, telling him simultaneously to dig, that they have forgotten him, that he ought to take care of himself, that he ought to give his life for his country, that he's a good soldier, that he's worthless.

The soldier erases the faces with one blow. All of them. And alone there in the pit, as if it had swallowed him up, his body shakes as though something were battering it from inside. He gives out noises like small thunderings but higher pitched, more animal. His mouth stretches and twists into a grimace like a theater mask. His eyes close, squeezed tight, and from them some drops fall, as they did from his fingers before.

He continues not looking at the clouds of his thoughts. He just lets it rain, cleaning everything the way the forest is cleaned.

It rains all night, while the soldier sleeps.

The next morning arrives, as always, over the plain and it is magnificent, feminine.

It sneaks into the forest to look for the soldier and it caresses him. The soldier feels there's something new in the air, and thinks that perhaps today is the day they'll come for him.

He has moved the position of his encampment several

times so as not to waste time walking to the far end of the ditch.

The grub is a snake that has extended itself and now it separates the plain from the forest: it has taken on a meaning.

The soldier thinks perhaps they aren't coming back for him but instead he will be the one to reach the next digger as his own section proceeds.

"It's a good day," he tells himself as he eats. Once again he thinks that he'd like to eat fish. He decides to try it, to construct a kind of fence and put it in the stream.

In the forest there are plants that seem sufficiently long and flexible to be interwoven.

Knife in hand, he walks into the forest and into its magic.

When he walks into the forest he always feels like he's returning to something. Though they might be made of different plants, all forests are the same forest.

He walks looking upward in search of vines.

Suddenly a flash, a blow, a fire burning one of his legs. He falls to the ground, struck down. His shout drowns in his fear. He grips his leg with both hands, squeezes it beneath his left knee. He dares not touch it.

His body falls still. His mind too. The forest disappears.

When he wakes night has fallen, and he sees his mother multiplied among the trees. Something roars in the distance: inside the soldier. He drags himself away.

He remembers: he's wounded. Something must have bitten him. He imagines the venom running through his bloodstream. He takes off his shirt and ties it tightly at his knee. He thinks he ought to have done this earlier. The wound is small: two holes. "A snake," he thinks.

A snake like a ditch.

He tries to get up but feels dizzy. He crawls on hands and knees, like a dog.

Inside the shelter he allows himself to drop. He reaches for his canteen, drinks, and wets his head.

The world has turned strange, and it is threatening. He himself is a stranger in a body that burns.

His mother looks at him silently with eyes that are filled with words. The soldier takes the knife and tries to open his mother's eyes, but she shifts from place to place like a ghost. During that stationary pursuit inside the trench, he makes a cut in his hand.

He falls into sleep as into a trap. The prison-eyes of his mother multiply, they make holes in the darkness and peer straight at him.

The soldier spends one long night or several tossing and turning inside the trench. He clears the bottom of it and carves out a hollow in the shape of an egg, then curls up inside it like a zero. Though he tries to stop his hearing, like a dog lowering its ears, the shouts are coming from his chest. He closes himself off both on the inside and on the outside, he barely exists.

Something remains, and it hurts.

The only thing that's real is the water he drinks, and the fluids that come out of his body. And the pain that comes and goes like a wave, and drags him off, and spits him out onto a dream shore.

What will happen to the pit if he dies. Who will continue with the task. He tries to head that way, but the slope carries him someplace else: images of his mother, his friends, the rice fields, and the mountains. There's joy in this procession, as if death were smiling. A smile is always a shelter. The soldier falls asleep.

The following morning his own life is restored to him: the fever has gone, he's able to move.

His hunger is a welcome to the world of the living. He has a wounded hand. He washes and makes himself a bandage.

He opens the box of rations he'd kept in reserve and realizes what he has eaten during the days of his fever. Not many remain. He takes one and opens it.

The return of his superior officers has become vague.

The only thing that continues immovable inside and outside the soldier is the pit.

Perhaps they're all dead, he thinks. Perhaps the Japanese army has been decimated. Perhaps the enemy's. Perhaps what he's digging is a great big grave to bury the bodies. Thousands of them. Perhaps he will need to toss them all inside and then drop in as the final body himself.

When he finishes his portion of food he goes to take a look at the pit.

As soon as he sees it, he recognizes it: to one side the plain, to the other, the forest.

This pit is him, himself: something that divides, sinks, grows.

Made of mud and lack. Full of dead bodies.

He remembers suddenly what it was that he'd buried when he was a little boy. A stick that one of the rice-field owners used to carry around. It seemed to him to be a symbol of command. The memory nudges something. He doesn't know what was in his mind as he did it. He remembers what he felt: a weight. "Obedience," he thinks, and the word illuminates what it shows.

As on other occasions, without realizing it, he has begun to dig and is surprised to find himself in the middle of the task.

He remembers the red X and Captain Takeda. He remembers the day he joined the army. He was happy, filled with pride, ready to die. He had turned eighteen a few days earlier. A uniform, a weapon, a mission, all these seemed to be his gifts. The gifts that the emperor was sending to the last of his subjects, the smallest, the son of a country widow in a little corner of the mountains. He had placed his life on a tray by way of thanks, and just stood there looking ahead, empty of anything that was not surrender.

Something settles into place.

Like tea leaves that have stretched into the heat of the water.

The slow fall restores their essence: a green scent. On one side and on the other, they drop down as if unwillingly. A fall that resembles a flight.

The bottom of the pit just waits. The leaves always arrive. He has stopped digging.

He comes out of the pit.

For the first time he would like to know what day it is. The name of the land he walks on.

He rushes to look for the mirror he once used for shaving, and with it he looks for himself.

The mirror is small: he goes over his face bit by bit, like a patch of terrain.

Beneath his cheekbones, his beard begins: on one side his skin clean as a plain, on the other a dark forest of hair. But it's the look in the eyes that loses him: it's somebody else.

He returns to one side of the ditch.

Standing on one of the mounds protecting it, he raises the spade, fills it with earth, and tips it out into the void.

The depth is unaltered. The soldier's action causes no change.

The soldier feels invisible. He takes more quick spadefuls, shoving the earth into the pit.

He's going to fill it all up even if it takes twice the time and effort it took to dig it.

He throws earth into the pit for the whole day. He doesn't hunt, doesn't eat. He drinks a lot of water.

His thoughts float past and he tries to see their cloud shapes and decode them.

Mixed in among his memories, what returns to him is his name: Hyuga.

He remembers his mother calling him. Lying back onto the memory, which is so soft, he falls asleep. He dreams that the pit has teeth along its edges, metal ones.

The night transforms what it touches.

When the soldier wakes, his decision has become a question.

His answer is to spade in more earth.

Finally he knows what it is that he's burying: he is burying the pit. He's going to make it disappear beneath the earth.

He toils hard.

Suddenly he feels a trembling in the air, deep and soft. Something roars, approaching. A plane.

Hyuga's heart rejoices. They've come for him. But an avalanche of thoughts crashes down upon his joy.

He is disobeying. He is filling in the ditch that he has been ordered to dig. He is attacking General Imagawa's order and jettisoning the career of Captain Takeda who chose him for the task. He is clearing a path for the enemy. He is betraying the emperor. He will be tried, convicted, and executed dishonorably.

What's a man good for, if not to serve the good of his country?

A man without a country is a link without its chain, a loose piece, a single drop too small to wet anything.

The airplane has gone.

They haven't come to fetch him. They haven't attacked him. Something happened as though nothing had happened.

The earth is no longer trembling. The pit seems to look at him.

He continues to refill it. He hopes his mother will understand. He is an insect coming out from underneath a rock. Death doesn't matter.

Something has turned. The honor is in disobedience.

He can't get the image of Sachiko out of his head.

She is as real as the air.

To die is to give her up. To die is never again to see the moon. That's what the dishonor would be, nothing else.

He throws the earth into the pit, returns it.

The bottom of the pit rises slowly as the days pass with Hyuga throwing spadefuls over it.

Still he does not hunt. For several days he reduces his food intake to one daily portion.

He can see his hands getting thinner by the day.

When he was a boy he looked at his feet. Now he looks at his hands. His hands on the spade's wooden handle, cupping to fill with water, pushing mounds of earth into the pit when he tires of working with the spade.

His hands are covered in calluses. Like the shells of turtles that are ancient, and good, and tired.

The days resemble one another as they did before, only now they are progressing toward a place that Hyuga can see: death. Seeing is important, it is knowing, mastering.

Death is no more than the earth falling onto the pit of life.

Calmly he sleeps and dreams about the mountain next to his town. He climbs.

At the top there is an abyss: the mountain is no more than a cone of rock surrounding a hole.

He falls. He wakes up.

The location of his first encampment approaches as Hyuga continues to make progress. The points of departure and of arrival are the same. A route in the shape of a circle.

He remembers the red X and remembers not having seen it.

He hopes his actions won't have consequences for anyone but himself. He is the link off the chain, the loose piece, the dead man.

The pit no longer divides anything. Its meaning recedes.

As if he were burying somebody whose face was now visible, it takes Hyuga greater effort to carry out the same strokes of the spade. The earth weighs heavily.

One morning, as if refusing to go on, the spade breaks. His companion becomes two useless pieces, one of metal, the other of wood.

Hyuga continues with his hands. His body's spades.

The large, deep ditch that split the earth is now a black hole big enough to fit a dog. One sole dog, ownerless.

Hyuga is on his knees, a hand resting motionless on each leg.

He throws fistfuls of earth into the pit. He doesn't think about death, he feels it, like a certainty. A certainty is a firm thing: it sustains. Hyuga leans in, rests on this idea.

When the pit has been buried and all that remains is a black scar across the earth, Hyuga returns to the shelter and sleeps.

For several days planes fly overhead. As if they've been waiting for him to finish.

Days align with our time when we don't count them, thinks Hyuga.

He no longer swims in the flowing days: he floats, sinks, spins.

One morning, as he's putting his fish-catching barrier in place, he sees an old local man coming down the stream.

Two calm surprises. Hands that dance in a game of gesturing.

The old man recognizes the shreds of Hyuga's uniform and tries to explain something.

Hyuga thinks he understands that the war is over. Japan has lost.

The man, who looks like a hunter, tells Hyuga to follow him.

They arrive at a small village that seems only recently settled. The people have come from another of the islands, fleeing an epidemic.

He asks the date. Makes the calculation. He has been in the forest a long time.

If Hyuga's life were a bowl of rice, his time with the pit would be a sizable mouthful. Enough to leave Hyuga hungry if that part were taken from him.

After three days, two Japanese government officials show up to fetch him. They lead him back to his land.

Hyuga has no words. He does not explain his disobedience.

He will hear the army dissecting his story, and he will eat up the pieces in silence.

He spends the whole trip readying himself.

Once in Japan, he is taken in an army vehicle back to his town.

Three days later he is to present himself at the Army Central HQ.

Standing outside his house, he looks at it.

The sand on the roof is too heavy and there are places where the beams have given way. Twenty centimeters of sand to keep the house cool in summer and warm in winter.

A neighbor approaches. Hyuga greets him. The man looks without recognition.

Hyuga says he's the widow's son. "You've grown," says the man.

Hyuga says nothing.

Looking down, the man adds: "Your mother died."

The abyss that Hyuga saw in his dreams is now in his chest, in his mouth.

It grows. It overflows from his body, surrounding him.

The emptiness expands over everything, denying all of it.

The first day he goes through the house, cleans it, tidies. He finds his mother in the objects.

His meals are fish and rice.

He watches Sachiko from afar.

On the second day he buys wood and fixes the roof.

On the third day he travels to Tokyo and is billeted in a garrison alongside other soldiers. The following day he will be called to give evidence about his case.

In the barracks he tells his story.

Some are surprised, but there are many stories that come and go and Hyuga's is lost. The talk is no longer about enemies but victors.

Hyuga asks after General Imagawa: he died on the island, during a raid.

About Captain Takeda he is unable to discover anything at all.

That night he doesn't sleep. The following morning he is called.

A large room in which there is only a desk and behind it an officer who does not give his rank. On the desk, piles of forms.

Hyuga states his rank, says he was part of the squadron based on the island, and that his mission was to dig a pit.

Then he is silent for a moment, filling his chest with air and strength.

The officer interrupts him: "How d'you spell your name?"

Hyuga answers.

The officer asks who was leading the squadron.

Hyuga names Captain Takeda.

The officer doesn't look up from the forms he is filling.

Hyuga, filled with bravery, confesses.

The officer repeats: "You refilled the pit you dug?"

"Yes," says Hyuga from deep inside himself. The officer says nothing.

Hyuga thinks about the calmness of storms as they advance across the plain. No brashness, no mercy or pause.

Hyuga waits to be led to a cell.

The officer looks at Hyuga as though not seeing him and says he can withdraw.

Hyuga asks permission to speak and repeats what he has done. The officer looks tired. He says the war is over, their duty now is to rebuild. He returns to his forms.

Hyuga remains standing in front of him, in silence. "What are you waiting for?" says the officer, annoyed. Hyuga leaves the room.

His cap in his hand. Slow steps, almost motionless, toward the street.

His eyes move as though searching for something. Short quick flights like a restless insect.

Outside there are no clouds. A sky in silence.

A woman and a little girl are carrying pots and pans. They are running. Hyuga's eyes go on searching and do not find. A soldier passes on a bicycle. He has an open parasol on his head. Three circles: the parasol and the wheels.

The bicycle recedes into the distance, drawing a viper on the earth. Hyuga's eyes settle.

They come to rest on the track that has been left. More people go by.

A hint of the viper still remains on the earth. It is erased.

OUT IN
THE DARKNESS

Beneath its lid the eye is always open

CÉSAR FERNÁNDES MORENO

I stood in the elevator until somebody came in and asked which floor I was going to. I'd forgotten to press the button.

I walked into the apartment and sat down. When my handbag came to rest on the armchair, the strap slipped off my shoulder and fell slowly and silently onto the blue depths of the cushions. I don't know how long I stayed like that. As if sitting on a riverbank. And like a log borne past me on the flowing water, time brought the idea of remaining in darkness. I clung to that idea. I lowered the blinds, shut the curtains, turned out the lights.

Darkness is never perfect. Light is its defect. I tied a black blindfold over my eyes and remembered: "Beneath its lid the eye is always open."

Just a few days after moving in, I thought that the first thing I heard in my new apartment would determine what my days there would be like.

The movers' baskets had been taken away, and as if my voice had previously been warmed amid the zigzagging of all the wicker, as if the remnants of those baskets' plant life had heard me but then the walls had refused to do the same, now my voice bounced blankly against them, cold.

I searched the records that were still on the floor for Liszt's transcription of Beethoven's Sixth Symphony played by Glenn Gould.

The gray hands in the photograph looked like spiders and I could see them on the keys while I listened. Spiders moving slowly, as if on the prowl.

But the sounds of your music came in from the balcony and tangled up with mine like streamers: they fell.

Then I turned up the volume. You lowered yours. The following day I copied you.

We exchanged music via the balcony for a few days.

We shared a balcony that opened to the rear of the building with a dark pane of glass in between to separate your space from mine.

Our block was the tallest in the area, as if it had stood up and the others had not.

Two or three days after beginning our dialogue through music, I went out onto the balcony and walked over to the glass. I sensed you were there, I don't know if I heard you breathe or make some movement.

"I do like this landscape," I said, and it was true.

I liked what could be seen from the balcony, it had been the main reason I'd bought the apartment.

It was as if the city that imposed itself so vertically when you were on the street, vertical as a hierarchy, here became gentle, laid out at the balcony's feet, offering up its roofs and its terraces like disloyalties and secrets.

"I like the air," you said, and I was unsettled by your voice, your woman's voice.

I'd imagined you male and in my thoughts had called you "the guy next door." Your voice was like playing a C on a keyboard and hearing a G.

I didn't answer.

For a few days we proceeded with only the music. From Beethoven we moved on to Satie, and from his piano solo to one by Bill Evans. From him to Keith Jarrett, first with double bass and drums and then doing the Goldberg Variations, which inevitably returned us to Glenn Gould, where we had begun.

Later I discovered that all our conversations would take that form: a circle. A full moon, a zero, the Earth, a maternal belly, an egg. This was the shape our words drew when we conversed. They would return of their own accord to where they had begun. I never understood what it was that guided them, but they moved with certainty, like ants. And just like when I was a girl and I'd tried to modify the paths of ants by placing obstacles before them or throwing water on them, in our chats I would sometimes attempt small diversions that never worked.

I suppose ideas have a tendency to draw circles because if they didn't, if they just lined up one after another, they'd get lost in infinite straight lines, never getting anywhere.

Thus, in circles, I gradually showed you my whole life through the glass, or rather just its essence, hidden in details, tones, symbols. My son, fifteen years of marriage, the second child who never came, crisis, divorce, starting work at thirty-five, discovering photography.

As I told you these facts, my words threw light on them and I could see them differently. My life as a path to lead me to where I was at this moment. I wouldn't have understood any of this if you hadn't been on the other side of the glass.

I walk through the living room, which in the dark is enormous and not my usual one. I feel for the button on the sound system and put on some music. A piano, then a violin and a cello. The music is clearer in the dark. I can feel what I cannot see.

After we had talked several times with the glass between us, it seemed discourteous not to invite you to my place or introduce ourselves face to face somehow.

One day, in the elevator, a woman took a little while to press the floor where she was going. I wondered if that was the face of the voice, of your voice. Her face added nothing, rather it got in the way between the balcony voice and me. Any face would have gotten in the way.

"You'll think it strange," I said to you later on the balcony, "but I'd rather we didn't see each other, that we went on talking without seeing each other."

You replied immediately that there was no need for us to see each other, and our agreement was made.

The first few times I would sit on the balcony and wait. I didn't know what for, but I did know that what I was doing was a waiting: sitting, opening my chest, and watching time pass.

We began to agree on a schedule without ever talking about it.

That's what many of our agreements were like: a thing that simply comes to its own terms. Like a body that makes sand take its shape by shifting gently in it. I would sit in my chair and wait for you. Like now, seated on the kitchen chair in the dark.

A while back I saw a painting by Nora Iniesta. I told you about it. Three black chairs, with no curves or peculiarities, four legs and a rectangle bent into a right angle. They were shown face on, equidistant and parallel.

The picture produced no sensation in me until a few days later I saw a drawing by Agdamus of three chairs forming a scalene triangle, disordered. It was obvious there was something human about this: a conversation, a bit of time shared, discussions or plans. At that moment I realized that in the first picture nothing had happened. Or if anything, just a misunderstanding or a silence.

Chairs are magical objects.

Something happened to my chair, the one that was next to the glass on the balcony. It was an armchair, really. It had arms which did not embrace you but supported you with wooden firmness. My chair transformed into something new, it lost its chair's innocence after that pact between your voice and me.

As we talked I would look at the landscape, and when sometimes as a reflex I would turn my head to look at you, it was my own face I'd see reflected in the glass.

I didn't know your face, but I knew beyond it.

The darkness in the house now is smooth. There are small noises that walk across it like insects. I feel the cold of the water I drink and I feel my own tongue, my throat, like something that opens and closes, my hair tickling my shoulders, my weight.

I walk over the cold floor tiles, past the purring of the fridge, over to the door to the living room. My steps have shortened.

Walking from one darkness into another is like entering nowhere at all. But in my feet I feel the almost soft warmth of the wood, the yarn of the rug.

The absence of colors is a kind of silence. I run my hands over the armchairs, the coffee table, some ornaments, a book I've left lying about. My head slightly raised, as if trying to look further and over something. I recreate in my memory the pictures of these objects I know. Then I try to imagine them being only what I touch, what I smell, what I hear, not what I see.

What are they, each of the things that are? A stone, for example, its slow temperature, its hardness, its singular shape. A butterfly? The fluttering, the air moving in tiny waves.

Which things would seem beautiful to me if I could not see them? The sound of water, certainly, music. I think of scents and tastes. I think about your voice. Your voice was serene, just slightly rippling, transparent. I learned to recognize shades in it that words cannot catch, the way we recognize the steps of somebody we're expecting or the particular way they turn the key when they open the door.

Several times I said that I like the landscape and on each occasion you asked me to describe it to you. Once I talked to you about the dirty sky that crushed the city, another time about the windows that were beginning to light up like waking eyes. Another time I paused on a crack in a building opposite us: a quiet lightning bolt splitting the wall. I had liked the idea that, even without moving, the lightning bolt could be true to its essence and split the wall.

You listened attentively and asked questions that always revealed something. You revealed things, ideas, whole worlds, through your questions. You almost never gave answers, only new questions. Questions that were serene, with no great eagerness, without the greed that some questions have for answers, as if they cannot be alone. Your questions seemed like answers.

The city was changing before us, like a great show. So many skies went past, so many different cities…

When it rained, we couldn't go out onto the balcony, but the cold didn't stop us, not unless it was really bad. I remember sitting down with my hands in my pockets, my hood up, and a steaming cup at my side.

In spring and summer our conversations lengthened and we even crossed the threshold of midnight still talking.

What time must it be.

In the darkness, time becomes disordered, it doesn't catch hold of things. Space meanwhile expands. And fear too. Noises take on new meanings, like when we walk through a cemetery. We are more alone. Mirrors are extinguished. Darkness is the land of monsters. But there's no need to hide. Nor is it even possible. It's a kind of exposure, being out in the darkness.

You asked me about my job as a photographer. I took photos at schools, baptisms, weddings, parties. At first I'd wanted to capture this detail, that little gesture, but unconsciously over time I came to learn that sometimes the thing I was trying to show was the very thing people wanted to conceal.

I had the sense there was something you weren't saying. But who doesn't have secrets, who doesn't just give their own versions of things? Who doesn't reveal themselves also in what they hide of themselves?

All us women have a secret, ever since we were little girls. No matter what it's made of, it constitutes us, just as we are constituted of waiting and silence.

You talked about a childhood in the countryside. A move to the city for school. A career as a music critic. A few love affairs. But all these things seemed mere details when we sat on the balcony facing out toward the landscape.

It was as if we were playing with a flashlight and a magnifying glass. We would shine a light on some thing or other and look at it together, and then suddenly there we were, you and I, in whatever we were looking at.

On the balcony, that space that is both inside and outside at once, we talked about details. We are in them, like the DNA in every cell.

"The way you look at things," you said one day on the balcony. In taking those photos, I had lost my way of looking at things. So then I chose a subject: women aged forty, in their homes.

When I finished the first series, I put the photographs into a brown envelope and slipped it between the wall and the balcony glass, the same gap through which we had exchanged copies of our apartment keys, to show them to you.

You said nothing.

I called up each of the women, and, appealing to the bond that we'd formed in taking the first photos, I asked if we might repeat our session. I did a second series that turned out better than the first. I slipped the envelope between the wall and the glass and waited.

Still you made no reference to them. You did ask me, though, what the women were like and we talked about each one.

I repeated that series several more times, with as many women as chose to stick with it. I would slip the envelopes between wall and glass, and I would wait.

As had happened with the painting of the chairs and then the drawing, I never noticed what was missing from the first photos till I saw the last ones.

Sitting on the balcony opposite a colorless city and sky, I went through each of the photos on my lap, describing them to you.

In one of them was my solitude, in another the kind of aging I fear, the madness that sometimes rears its head, my anxieties, my vulnerability, my strength.

When I told you this, you said the work was good. I am comfortable in the darkness. I see things I imagine.

A very old god creating man. He shapes him from mud and breathes into him. And finally he ties a little piece of darkness to his feet that he calls "shadow."

The darkness has become welcoming.

You disappeared as softly as you had arrived, with no explanations, like spring and winter. And just like a body that makes sand take its shape by shifting in it, your absence became a space in my life.

Until one day, arriving home, I saw the neighbors standing on the sidewalk.

They were talking about your having left. And one of the women called you "the blind lady." The other nodded, as if everyone knew you were blind. Then they went on complaining about the weather. I greeted them with a simple nod of the head. I stepped into the elevator and just stood there until somebody came in and asked which floor I was going to. I'd forgotten to press the button.

I take the keys to your apartment from out of the second drawer in the kitchen. I've never used them. I let myself into your apartment, and do not turn on the lights. On the balcony there are several plant pots. The plants are brown, but they retain the shapes of branches filled with leaves and a few flowers. As if death has taken them by surprise.

Between the wall and the glass are the envelopes, all closed, just lightly resting on the soil of one of the pots.

I return home, part the curtains, raise the blinds, open the balcony's glass doors. My chair is alone.

I close my eyes and feel the air. What you could see, I can see now too.

THE HEADSCARF
AND THE WIND

The last times didn't count. They'd been at those parties where my sisters did whatever they could to get us all together, as if that way we'd be the family we used to be, as if all you needed to make an orchestra was to assemble some musicians in the same place. But no, those times didn't count. The last ones for me had been the same ones they'd been for her, those summers, otherwise she wouldn't have asked me if we could spend three days together in the country like before. "All of us?" I'd asked her on the phone like an idiot. "No," she'd said, "no one else. I want things to be nice and calm, everybody would be a lot of people." That's what I was thinking about when I saw her at the station, or rather, when I recognized her way of walking, as if nothing were weighing her down, neither her body nor time nor that thing we all accumulate the way you accumulate old bits of junk in a cupboard you never open.

Lala, I thought, the sweetest one, the gentlest. "Laura," I said, and I walked over. Then I realized. She was wearing a headscarf and under it there were no traces of Lala's straight shiny dark hair. She'd always had the sort of slightness that made you see the elegance of a deer in her fragility, like a flower with few petals or the very finest branches on a tree. But now, standing on the platform, with a small bag at her feet, a blue scarf on her head, eyes bigger than ever, her thinness was that of something ending, something you describe with the word less, whatever it is that things have about them when they move away. The impulse to hug her faded in the space between us and my open arms dropped to my sides. I know now that what I needed at that moment was words. I just ran my eyes up and down her, and she said: "Auntie didn't tell you anything?" Everything inside me was falling and I wasn't quick enough to catch it. My mom's voice saying: "María Laura is sick," talking about "this thing with María Laura" in a very low voice, and me letting the words just pass me by the way I sometimes do with my mom.

"You hadn't heard," said Lala, and I couldn't even answer no. "Better that way," she says, "it means you came because you wanted to. I'm glad about that." And then she was Lala again, my cousin, the one I had wanted to hug before. I put my arms around her shoulders, clumsily and now ill-timed, and she hugged me back and said I was an idiot. "The very same as always," I said, "just so you'd be able to recognize me."

We got in a taxi outside the station and asked to be dropped at the edge of town. We walked. I thought then that I understood what Lala wanted: on this dirt track, between acacias, I was once again five years old, eight, eleven, fourteen, twenty.

The house was waiting for us as that house always seemed to be. Funes and his wife kept it up, not too clean, not too dirty, tidy, and, as they said, always "ready," and that was how the house awaited everybody, with objects collected since the start of the century, the last century, superimposing renovations from the seventies, the nineties, as well as some I'd not seen before.

There was an exceptionally old iron hammock in which we used to swing, all eleven cousins together. Among the willows there was a marble table, around which we used to put cement benches decorated with bits of colored ceramic, a few chairs made of red wire, others of wicker, like for the beach, and a single chair in iron standing alone. It was wonderful to see all those pieces together as witnesses of the times the house had been through, gathering up this and that on a whim to bear it all to the present like a loving, ridiculous offering. The dishes, for example—there were Limoges ones with blue and gold edges, Rigolleaus with orange and pink flowers, plastic plates, crockery, cracked ones, brown glass, soup dishes for kids that Lala and I had once used. There were four different juicers. In the bedrooms there was a smell of damp despite Funes's wife opening the shutters every week. There were crucifixes over several beds, picture frames scattered all about the house. There were even people we didn't recognize in those photos. Some were of us on a day we'd forgotten. There were dogs, there were always a lot of dogs in that house, this time there were seven. Tiny ones and huge ones, all of them mixed breeds. When I was a little boy I'd tried to figure out whose they were, if they were Funes's, this being Funes Senior in those days, or ours. "They're the land's," my dad had said, "the dogs belong to the land."

"But what about the land," I'd said, "the land is ours, though, right?" My dad had laughed and said to me: "The things that are the land's belong to the land, Juan, they're not anyone's."

Lala asked Funes's wife the names of the new dogs, and then they all crowded around her happily, as if even the ones who didn't know her had understood who she was. Lala, who as a little girl always used to let the dogs into her bed.

We spent the afternoon in the house, playing around with memories, laughing. "Now we have memories," said Lala. "Before, when we were kids, we didn't. But Juan," she said, "we do have this."

"And we're making new ones," I said and even as I spoke I regretted it. Then I got up and said: "I'd better go cook something." I asked Funes for the keys to the truck and went into town. I found less than I'd hoped for, but it was enough. I swung by Amparo and bought wine, oil, spices, poppy seeds, and black and white sesame. I'd asked Funes for a chicken and some vegetables, "whatever there is," I'd said.

Lala had put the stereo in the kitchen. Marvin Gaye tapes, Beatles tapes.

While I cut the vegetables, I realized that there, in that country kitchen, was the reason I had devoted myself to cooking. I had learned to love those smells before I learned to talk. Lala said this place explained what she was too. Then she said she was going to fetch something and she went.

Each time she left me alone a whole pack of ideas would circle around me and only Lala's presence would be able to dispel them again. I emptied my glass and poured myself another, I gulped it as if I were pouring the wine into my body, I wiped my mouth with the back of my hand as I never would have done in front of Lala.

When she came back, with a little bunch of jasmine, I wanted to tell her not to leave me alone, but I knew she'd say that I was an idiot. I set the table, and, with a dishcloth in the crook of my elbow, my feet together, I served her what I had cooked. We ate with music and when a song came on that made Lala start to sing I got to my feet, turned up the volume, and danced.

I danced like I did when I was twenty. She told me I'd always been like that. "Like what?" I said. "Alluring," she said. I got up onto the chair and went on dancing for her, lifting up my T-shirt, spinning with my eyes shut. Lala laughed and I would have done anything for her to keep on laughing just like that. The chair seemed to be dancing with me, obedient. When I fell, Lala ran over and put her hand under my head. I felt like she'd done this many times, each time I'd fallen from a tree, each time any of us had been thrown by a horse or gotten a scolding. Lala's big eyes, her pale skin. She had a small hollow in her forehead, as if someone had made a mark on her. I felt like we all owed her something. I closed my eyes and moved toward her face. "What are you doing," she said and pushed me away. "What are you doing," she said again with fury in her eyes. "I don't know," I said, then watched her leave the kitchen. I know now that I'd have wanted to ask her what I should do, because despite not managing on that weekend to do what she wanted, I was up for anything. I would have done whatever she asked me. But Lala never asked for anything.

That night I went off to the large bedroom at the other end of the house. What should I do? Talk to Lala about God? Decrucify those Christs that had been perpetually dying over our beds since we were kids? Make her happy for one weekend, save her from the succession of simulations of happiness that her life sometimes seemed to me? Is there such a thing as mediocre happiness? I've always felt I didn't know how to cry, as if there was a correct way of doing it. I cried flat on my back with my arms at my sides, like when I was a kid, giving myself up to the very last resources. I cried myself to sleep.

In the morning Lala had put flowers on the table and prepared breakfast. Home-baked bread, butter made by Funes's wife, milky coffee in big mugs, an egg. She was very calm. She asked me what it was like being a cook on a boat, if I was happy, if I was in love. I didn't dare ask her the same questions. She talked to me about her garden, said she never could have lived on a boat because she couldn't have a garden. She said she missed working and she smiled. Sometimes she smiled just to make things easier for the rest of us.

Then we went out for a walk. The memories kept on falling gently onto Lala and me, as we allowed ourselves to travel through them as though it was we who were the ghosts and not all those surrounding us, those cousins, uncles, aunts, grandparents, and children who enveloped us in a quiet murmuring beneath the sun or between the trees. We strolled round to the far side of the lagoon and there we saw the horses. "Look, Laura, it's Morita," I said. "Can't be." "Yeah, look, the way she just stepped, that marking on the side of her face. It's Morita." "Morita must have died, Juan." "Why must she? Nobody has to die." "They do, Juan," said Lala and we fell silent. The countryside, the lagoon, and the afternoon too. When we asked Funes he said the mare was Morita's daughter and she had all the same tricks. "And all her same virtues no doubt," said Lala. Funes laughed and said he'd saddle her up if we wanted. "Yes, Funes, we'll go out tomorrow morning," said Lala. I'd been thinking about what they must have done with Morita when she died. I couldn't imagine Funes performing any kind of ceremony for a horse. I didn't ask and I said to Lala, yeah, going out in the morning was a good idea.

The hours passed, between walking and memories. Lala would look out at the fields in silence and I wanted to see what her eyes saw. We returned home in the evening and I made us something to eat.

"Let's go out tonight," I said. "You want another walk, when it's nice and quiet out there?" she asked. "Nah, to fucking *run riot* out there." Lala never said bad words, but this time she laughed, and her laughter was different, shaking her head side to side and throwing it up spiritedly. This was something new in her and being new I thought it was good. "Up into the hills," I said. "All that way? At this time?" she said. "We've got all night." "Well, not all night," she said, "I do want to get some sleep." I don't know what expression my face made but she finally said: "Oh OK, go on then," and we took out the truck.

When the dirt track ended, we walked and then started to climb. Lala got tired and we sat down on a rock. The further up we went, the stronger the wind. "I want to show you something," I said. "The plank?" "How do you know?" "You got in trouble for coming here and you told me, Juan, don't you remember?" I didn't remember that, but I did still know how to get to the place where the hills seemed to offer up a diving board, a flat rock sticking out over the void that as a kid I'd named "the plank" after the planks on pirate ships. It had barely changed, it didn't stick out as far as in my memory, and it had sharpened slightly, but there it was, my favorite spot, my possibility for real risk at a time when everything was safe and I was scared all the same.

I climbed up and walked along the plank with arms wide. The wind made me press my body forward as though leaning on it and on the idea that it would not stop blowing.

"Juan, come down," said Lala, "you could fall." I shouted and my shout seemed to go backward, as if swept away, lasting no time at all. When I came down I said: "Your turn." "You're crazy," she said. I insisted and she said she wanted to go. "Lala, nothing's gonna happen to you," I was saying. "You and I want different things, Juan," she said finally and began to walk down through the rocks, alone. I followed her.

At the bottom, where the wind no longer blew, in the darkness and before starting up the truck, I thought I could hear the noise made by the moon as it moved, as if it were scraping against a metal sky, as if something was not right in this night where we happened to find ourselves.

The next morning the horses were tied up next to the porch.

As we were having our coffee Lala said: "Afterward, when we get back, we should pack our bags." "Let's stay one day more," I said. She said she couldn't. I insisted, and she looked at me without answering. "One night at least," I begged her. "I can't," she said, leaving the slice of bread on her plate, untouched.

By mid-morning we had arrived at the furthest paddocks, and when we were on our way back Lala began to gallop. She put the reins under one of her thighs and shouted: "Look no hands," the way Pichi, the youngest of the cousins, used to do, because she didn't know how to let go of the handlebar of her bike, and one afternoon she thought letting go of the reins was the same thing. "No hands," Lala was shouting, with that same spirit she'd laughed with before, "no hands." The mare galloped, stretching her neck forward as if she were swimming and didn't want to drown. The scarf flew off her head, and Lala was the most beautiful woman I'd ever seen in my life. She seemed naked, rising and falling on invisible waves, laughing completely. She didn't stop laughing and I followed her, galloping alongside, trying to say: "Look no hands," with the reins in my mouth, so that she'd keep laughing and galloping just the same.

We galloped almost the whole way back and when we reached the acacias, now down to a walking pace, Lala

said: "You know, Juan, Funes is wrong. You're right. This
is Morita. You can't get two markings that are identical,
and this marking is Morita's. And did you see how she let
me change rein whenever I did this? That's something only
Morita could do." I said yes, that was her mare, Morita, the
same Morita who had been here always.

PARTING

I'm up before the sun. I walk barefoot through the house and sit at the window. Summer is departing.

Now, everything seems still. Like footsteps, something seems to beat.

Departing. I pluck out a single syllable, *part*, to get a good look, turning it every which way like a cube.

On one side, I see my dad, in a kimono, packing suits.

The cases are leather and they have belts for straps. The walls are rice paper with sliding doors. I can see the whole scene. It is gentle.

I turn the cube and think about his departure, how that was not the moment he left Japan but when he decided to stay in Argentina. For me there's some other part missing from that scene. Something in that decision I don't understand.

I turn the syllable around and look again. "Parturition" is also the moment of arriving in life.

You know when the moment is right. Not through some doctor's calculations, but because as a woman you recognize it, the way you recognize somebody you've been waiting for as soon as their silhouette takes shape. Or sooner.

You accept what you feel. The doctor just hands you your date, as if handing down a sentence.

I decide not to go into work. I spend the whole day at home. I don't eat and I pace from side to side, like the lions in their cage. I am the lion and I am the cage enclosing him.

I think about my childhood.

I realized we were different when I went to school.

The other kids stretched out their eyes with their index fingers and called me "that Chink girl." I told them I was Japanese and they said same difference. I didn't answer. I didn't understand why they said that, nor lots of other things. They'd shout at me, push me, some of them hit me. All of them seemed very angry at me.

When I thought it was all over, that it had passed in the way an earthquake just passes, two boys who were bigger than me, in the boys' bathroom at school, made my brother cry. I never knew why they did.

From that day I started talking in the first-person plural.

Earthquakes are not only the trembling of the earth and one of the first words my dad learned to say. To Japanese people, they are a possibility.

They, the other children, were angry at us.

I said nothing about the behavior I used to see. Like how they never used to say thank you. As if things had always been where they found them, as if there hadn't been someone who'd placed them there to be found. Their food, their clothes, their toys.

They also left their shoes tossed about. They didn't place them in parallel like a pair of feet, out of the way and all lined up. Sometimes they'd be left sole upward and with their laces still tied, and it took them a while to put them back on.

Then I got to know their families and their homes. Those were different too. Either that or we were the different ones. I didn't know.

My favorite food was salmon roe. My dad would bring it back sometimes, from the boats. The other kids had never had it. They didn't know where Japan was either, and that there'd been a war outside of the movies.

As a teenager I got angry with the movies because they beautify war. That's not what war is like, I thought. When I asked my dad, he told me about the fear, he described the nights with blackouts and trying to hide in the darkness. Something tearing suddenly through the silence, growing. Then a procession of huge white birds. The noise is a vibration in the body. The silence shatters apart on the ground. He unfolds his arms. His eyes are very open and he looks at the sky outside that is light blue and he and I see black, sitting in the dining room at home. Those planes that came to drop bombs on them. He said they were beautiful. Terrifyingly beautiful.

I stop looking at the cubes of words and pictures.

My body is calling me.

I recognize one of the signs they taught me on the course. Now is the moment.

It is after 11 p.m. I make my calls, and my parents say they're heading over to fetch me. I'm calm, and I wait. I'm sitting in the living room of my house. The music that I put on is still playing. Bach. Some things are universal. Most of us follow more or less the same paths. With a few differences.

I don't have a TV. When I was a little girl I didn't have one either. By choice. It's hard to explain why one chooses certain things when you're doing it from a place where there are no words. When my dad was a boy he used to fall asleep looking at the grain of the wood in the beams of his house. TV isn't necessary. The cube shows another of its sides.

I go on waiting. Legs crossed in the lotus position, one hand above my belly and the other below. The future bursts into me and it is almost a reflex to look toward the past. My childhood is insistent: the other children never corrected their parents like I did, the way I sometimes told my parents that you say "children" not "childs," which they imagined was their plural. I adopted this place of difference as my own.

I did have to adopt someplace after all: the country where I lived considered me a foreigner, and the other country was one I wouldn't even have dreamed of going to.

Twenty years later I did go. And I was a foreigner there too. It hurt the way it hurts when you touch a wound. To suffer, love, and part, so says the tango. My dad had no interest in tango, nor in football. There is one side of the cube I cannot see, as if it were incomplete.

When I first encountered Japan, I was also meeting my dad. Not so much for what they had in common but for what sets them apart. A rebelliousness, meticulous and persistent, for example.

I pick up the cube and look at another side. To partition is to split in half, says the dictionary.

Half. In Japan that's what they call the children of a Japanese person with someone from another race.

In the past they used the word "ainoko," which means something kind of like love child, but after the war the word took on a derogatory burden because it was used for the children of Japanese women and US soldiers. Children of the enemy.

So I am *half*. I'm japanese in Argentina and argentine in Japan, with those small letters for me the Spanish way, and upper case for the countries.

A-part. As in—says the dictionary—to break apart. Another side of the cube. My dad left his mother in Japan, a widow since he was two, and his brother who'd been ill since the war.

My grandma was called Katsu and they say I look like her.

I only knew her through the stories my dad used to tell and a photo I once saw. I searched in it for the strong woman who supported her family on her own and her husband's family too, losing everything several times during the war.

The photo showed a little old lady who looked like one of those plums that in Japan they call "umeboshi." Small and wrinkled, uncomfortable in front of the camera.

Now, especially, they say I'm like her. Now that I'm going to have my own child alone. Alone at forty. They said I was "mature," which I think makes me sound like a tree. Trees are not born. They're not borne either, though they do bear. They stand strong, bearing. They bear fruit, and endure.

The way in which I feel most like a tree, more so now than at twenty, is in solidity. Some kind of strength.

One of the ways of saying strong in Japanese is Kenta. Such a beautiful word…

The pain comes, the one they've told me about. It bursts in and devours everything. I don't scream like in the movies. The house is silent.

My parents arrive, together, as they have been for forty-two years.

They married not long after meeting. My dad had only one guest at the wedding: an employee of the company he'd come over to work for. My mom, meanwhile, had hundreds, because they were in her town and it wasn't a big one.

Marrying a Japanese person was just about the weirdest thing you could do in Necochea. I read once that the most extreme form of intermarriage is marrying someone from another race.

Then they came to live in Buenos Aires. The office where my father worked was in La Boca, close to the port, where the little fishing boats he dealt with used to come in.

He had two bosses. For a Japanese person a boss isn't the same thing as it is for an Argentine. Hierarchies are deeply engraved. Order isn't a matter of whim, it's cast-iron. His bosses told him one day to bring his wife along for dinner with them. My dad told her the day and the time. They'd be waiting for her outside the agency. She took two subway trains and arrived six minutes late. Five minutes after the agreed time, the bosses said they were going to start walking to the place and that she should come whenever she showed up. My dad stayed behind to wait for her. She arrived just seconds later. The bosses were walking a few meters ahead and didn't turn around. My parents behind them. The bosses were offended by the delay, my mom by their manners.

My dad was between them, partitioned. Or multiplied. She was always with him. The way the walls of a house are always with the roof. She was always there almost invisibly, as she is in what I am writing here. And sometimes she seemed more Japanese than he was.

She measures the time between one pain and the next. My dad drives.

Lying back in the seat I see plane trees, tipas, maples passing by. The pain blurs them out. In their place it leaves a treeless desert.

To partition is to divide up. To divide is to know how many times one number fits into another.

How much fits into one. One, the point of departure. Everything fits in there.

My father chose to stay in this land for my mom, and other reasons. I try to find them.

He told me once that he stayed because of that bridge opposite the Law Faculty on Avenida Figueroa Alcorta, and because there is a forest in the south (in Bariloche, I think) where the trees that fall down don't get taken away but are left to be a part of the landscape.

The fallen trees are also the forest.

The idea of death was always different in my house.

It was not the opposite of life, but a part of it.

I could make a list of the words that had different meanings in my house from outside: death, I, winter, other, salt, effort, word, kiss, honor, grandfather, wait, tea, work, eat, silence, accept, pain.

The midwife says I can't possibly be having contractions already because if I were I'd be making more of a fuss. My mom says I don't make a fuss and she gives me her hand.

A lot of people complain about the weather. Never in my parents' house have I ever heard any complaints about the rain, the wind, the mist, the frost.

The midwife takes a look and partway through her checks she calls the anesthetist and the obstetrician as a matter of urgency.

I let go my mother's hand.

One hour later my baby is in my arms.

All I can say are the same few phrases that have already been said by every mother when they see their child.

The doctor is filling in a form without looking at me. "And the name?" he asks, turning to me now.

I look at my blood on the gloves he's still wearing. I search inside.

"Kenta," I reply.

I say the name one more time to give it to my son. Gentle and firm, I repeat: Kenta.

I feel like I am a part of something much bigger.

Something that began on the other side of the world, where people arrange their shoes neatly when they take them off, and which continues here, where people leave them any way they please.

AS BRIEF
AS A CLOVER

Three men yank hard on the hands of the foal so that it will finish being born.

It looks as though the mare's dying, so they send the kids into the house to watch TV. So they won't see the death.

To me, life, the birth of the foal, is no less gory than the mare's death would be. "Death is clean," I think.

The kids are scared but they don't want to leave. Vertigo floats in the air like a spiderweb, and they are caught, mute, still.

With something between a shove and a hug I bring them into the house and before long they seem to have forgotten the scene of the birth. Not me. I think about the mare and I remember the birth of my son.

The obstetrician and the anesthetist placed their forearms on my belly and threw all the weight of their huge bodies onto it. Each time they did it, streams of liquid fell onto the bare floor of the delivery room. Those waves of sound continue to strike the floor within my memory.

When the men return to the house from the shed they say the mare is fine, she's not dying.

The next day we go to see the foal. Twig legs ready to snap, soft fur, big eyes.

The ranch foreman picks it up and the kids take it in turns to stroke its belly: my two nieces, aged four and six, and my son, two.

Each one claims their place waiting in the short three-person line more than the actual touching of the foal, which passes fleetingly before they get back into the line saying: "Again, again…"

When the excitement abates, the man says they're off to feed the sheep, and the children run, laughing.

The dog barks as if she were laughing with them.

It's always like this: I'm just a mirror. The thing that stands there in the middle, forced to reflect. My son is happy: so am I.

No, it hasn't always been like this.

I had another life before him.

The foreman tosses a burlap bag onto the ground and tells the kids to gather some grass on top of it.

There is a new ram, a gift from a neighbor.

The foreman takes two corners of the bag and I show my son how to take the others.

They carry the grass over to the fence and throw it in the pen.

The sheep gather around the food, like all species do.

"They're so dumb," I think. Because of their meekness, because as they approach they're all glued to one another, because of what's missing from the look in their eyes.

The gate is open. "So dumb," I think again, as if they could actually escape to anywhere that wasn't just another captivity.

Now they're inside the pen. The dog goes in and someone shoos her away. The children run to the sheep. The trail of laughter sweetens the air and the dry earth. My son is wearing only a diaper. He raises his arms and shouts with his mouth open very wide. Everything in him is intense.

The girls meanwhile are cautious. The older one's awareness has grown like her legs have grown, and both of them, like all women, already have a secret.

They've corralled the sheep into one corner, next to the drinking trough.

The sheep bleat fearfully, clumsily. The children enjoy the power.

"Choose one," says the foreman, raising his lasso. He's going to rope the ewe so they can touch her.

You imagine sheep as being almost weightless and very white, with the density of a cloud. But the density of these animals is almost hermetic, they're heavy, ugly, their coloring dirty, all blacks and browns, smelling like something old.

My niece chooses a small one with a white mark on her head.

The foreman spins the lasso and catches the ewe's forelegs and she topples on her side, raising a cloud of dust.

The children run over to touch her with hands splayed. They touch her and I can feel the texture of the dry wool. I know they feel something that can only be supported by that act of touching: they have mastered what they used to fear.

They let her go and rope another. My son wants the lasso. He plays at throwing it, and when the chosen ewe is on the ground, the foreman lets him hold one end.

My son shrieks with delight and tugs on it hard.

I'm on the other side of the wire, outside the pen in which everybody is now running: the sheep, and behind them the children and the dog, and behind them the two men.

Suddenly the sheep are corralled into one corner, my nieces with them, the foreman behind, and my son is in the middle of the pen, alone, and another man at the other end, close to the gate.

And me, outside.

My son alone, barely a meter tall, milky legs, those impossible movements as if he has no muscles but is moved by some internal force, the way water moves, or wind.

I see him and I feel fear. A stab of fear. It's a thing that was born in me with him, this fear. A fear so real I can touch it the way I touch the wire. It has barbs.

I shout my son's name. He looks at me. He doesn't move.

The new ram splits off from the flock and runs toward him. Death is an animal that is running toward my motionless child. The ram gives a leap and brushes past him. The men run.

The foreman throws the lasso and misses. The other man shouts with his jaw dislocated. There are blue lines in his neck. They run differently. Everything has sped up. My nieces are crying. The ram turns around and once again it runs toward my son, head-on. The dog knocks my son off his feet, she lifts him up in a strange pirouette. He falls face down onto the earth. Everything happens fast and I run slowly, with all my strength. The foreman has roped the ram in mid-air. The ram also falls face down on the earth, bleeding.

I pick my son up from the ground. I hug him: I return him to my breast. He's crying. I run out of the pen and toward the house that has never been further away.

I feel liquid on my arms, I feel it sticky on my clothes. I hold my son out from me: his mouth is bleeding so much I can't even see it. Bleeding black blood. I press him toward me. I shouldn't have left him. No. I want to tear something from myself, I don't know which part. An arm, an eye, some entrails I've never seen, my name, something that hurts.

There's blood on my son's hands and on his face, on my chest, on our clothes. He looks at me with questioning eyes and I know I should answer that he's not to be scared. I squeeze him more tightly against my chest so he doesn't notice I'm trembling. I run. The house is still far away.

Before I get there, the women are already coming toward us. We all bustle inside together, with my son's crying at the center.

His questioning eyes are insistent each time he pulls away from my body.

I hold him next to the tap on the bath, the women wipe him clean with a cloth. They wipe blood and earth from his mouth. The same mouth that until recently only ever had milk from my breast.

I'm no longer trembling and it's less of a lie when I tell him it's all going to be OK. He's no longer crying. When I stop feeling scared, he calmly allows them to put on some ice. His lip is split, his frenulum just slightly torn, chin and forehead grazed. I tickle him and he laughs. He restores something to me, back to where it belongs. My son holds a small bag of ice up to his mouth. The world rights itself.

A short while later we're saying goodbye to the people who are heading out before the coming of the storm that is already announcing itself in the sky.

It's getting dark. But in the countryside, it isn't only light that's receding, lamps that are being lit.

As he passes, one of the men tells me quietly that he's ordered the ram to be killed.

The idea keeps me up that night, but in the moment I welcome it. The ram will die over and over as I toss and turn in my bed.

I will remember its tongue lolling from its open mouth onto the earth like something already dead or awaiting death.

"Don't kill it," I'll say in the morning. But at that moment, the idea of the ram's death comforts me.

I take my son in my arms, carry him outside. We are going to watch the storm.

We walk away from the house, until the windows are just yellow squares trembling.

The sky is vast, concave. It is not a light blue plane, flat and floating over porches and heads, it's something that encloses, inescapable, from far away.

"The sky is clean," I think. Something resounds. No, not the sky: death. "The sky is clean, but it's the earth that is beautiful," I think.

The storm announces itself in the silence and the wind.

Whatever announces itself in silence announces itself more powerfully. The horses run in circles, whinnying, warning.

The sheep bleat their wails and complaints. The birds fly as if fleeing.

My son notices the commotion, asks me if the storm is bad or good.

"We're going to see it," I tell him and point toward the south, which was previously orange and pink and before that was sky-blue. Now it's black.

To the east and the west, different blues.

Hugging in the middle of the field, as we watch what is to come, my son and I are as brief as a clover.